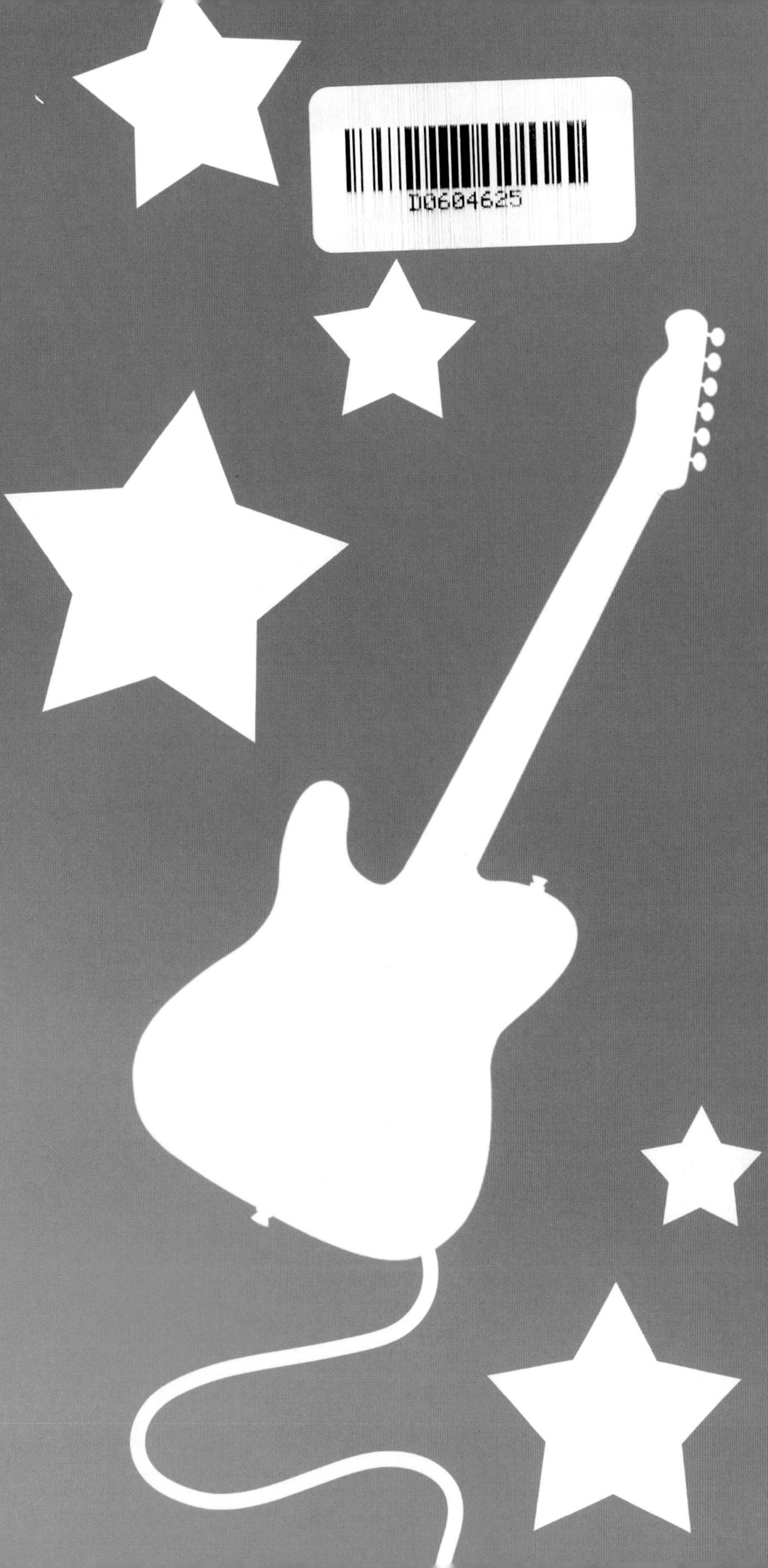

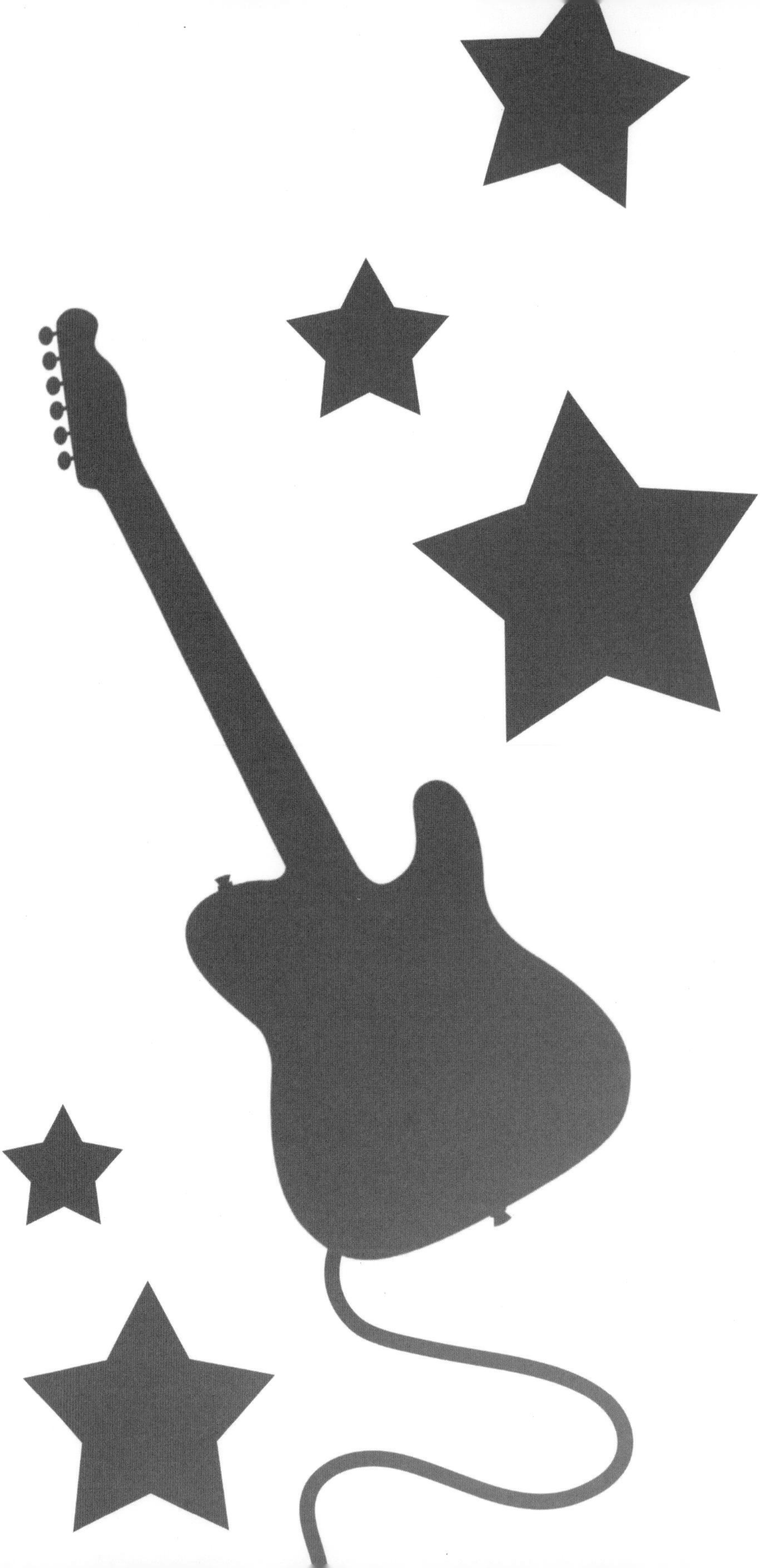

Pak • Coulton • Miyazawa
Kholinne • Bowland

# The PRINCESS who saved HERSELF™

Published by
kaboom!™

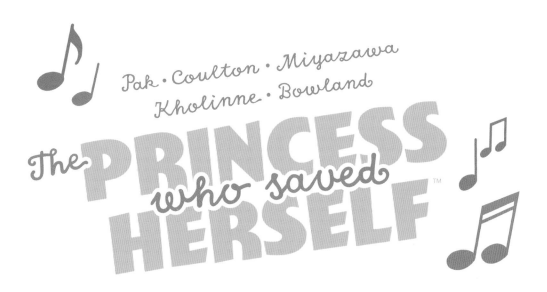

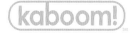

KaBOOM! Edition Editor
**Shannon Watters**

KaBOOM! Edition Assistant Editor
**Kenzie Rzonca**

KaBOOM! Designer
**Marie Krupina**

**THE PRINCESS WHO SAVED HERSELF, May 2021.** Published by KaBOOM!, a division of Boom Entertainment, Inc. Originally published as THE PRINCESS WHO SAVED HERSELF © 2015 Pak Man Productions, LTD. and 10 Print JoCo, Inc. KaBOOM!™ and the KaBOOM! logo are trademarks of Boom Entertainment, Inc., registered in various countries and categories. All characters, events, and institutions depicted herein are fictional. Any similarity between any of the names, characters, persons, and/or institutions in this publication to actual names, characters, and persons, whether living or dead, events, and/or institutions is unintended and purely coincidental. KaBOOM! does not read or accept unsolicited submissions of ideas, stories, or artwork.

BOOM! Studios, 5670 Wilshire Boulevard, Suite 400, Los Angeles, CA 90036-5679. Printed in China. First Printing.

ISBN: 978-1-68415-710-5, eISBN: 978-1-64668-248-5

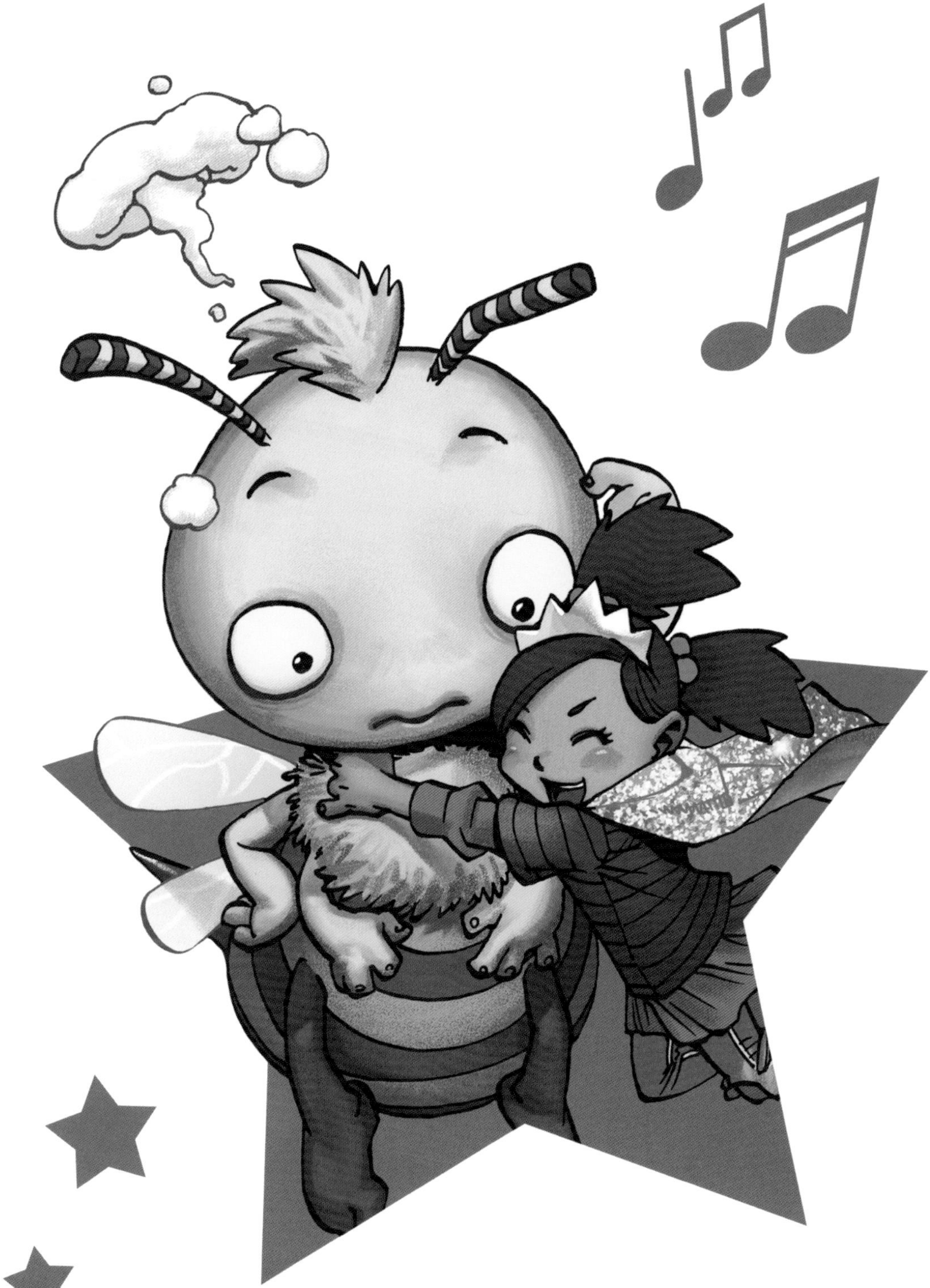

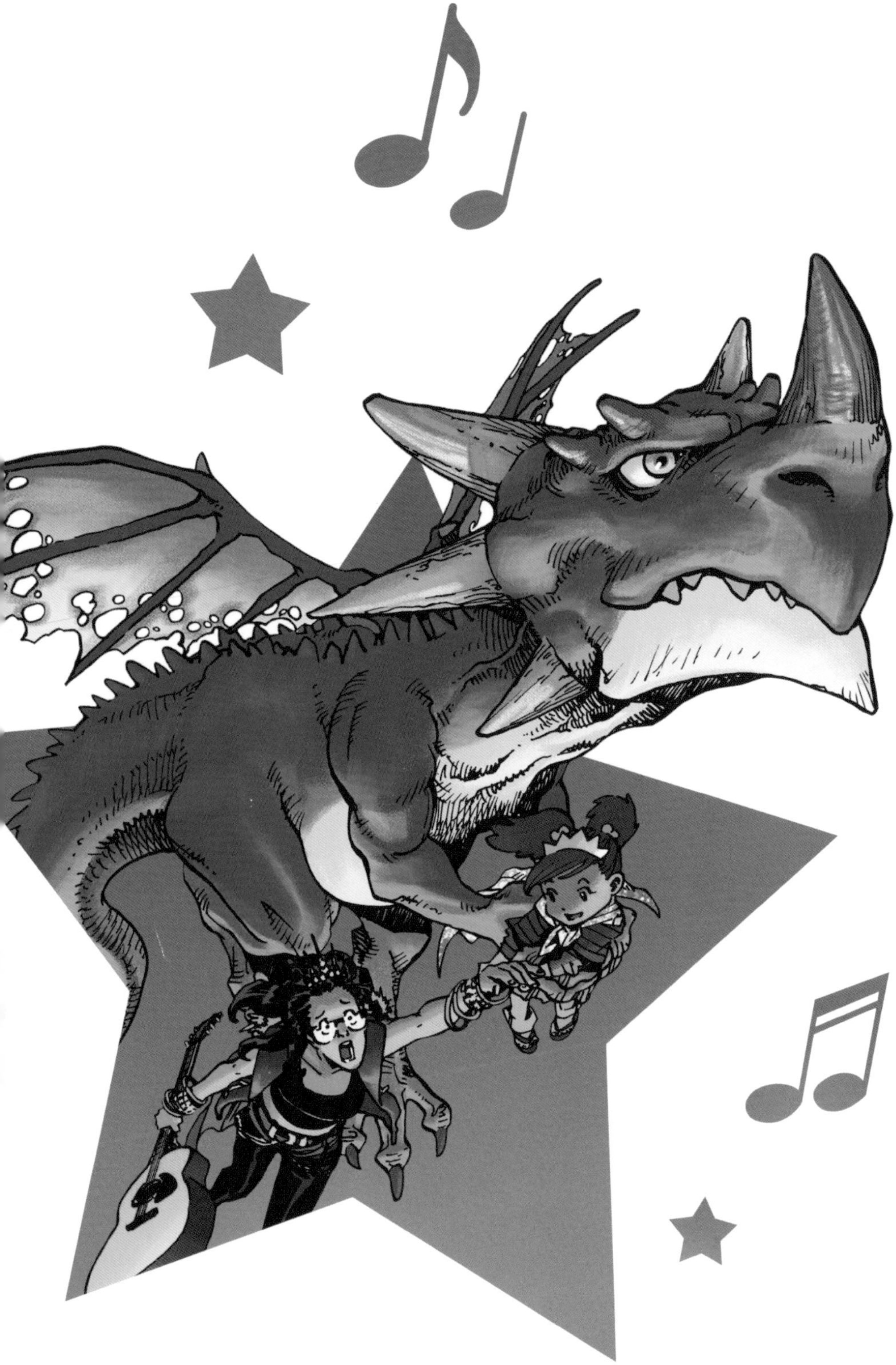

# The PRINCESS who saved HERSELF ™

Written by
## GREG PAK

Based on the song by
## JONATHAN COULTON

Art by
## TAKESHI MIYAZAWA

Colors by
## JESSICA KHOLINNE

Letters by
## SIMON BOWLAND

Once upon a time there was a princess named
Gloria Cheng Epstein Takahara de la Garza Champion

Who lived in a castle
by a waterfall

With a pink
and purple wall.

She had a
pet snake

And she ate a
whole cake...

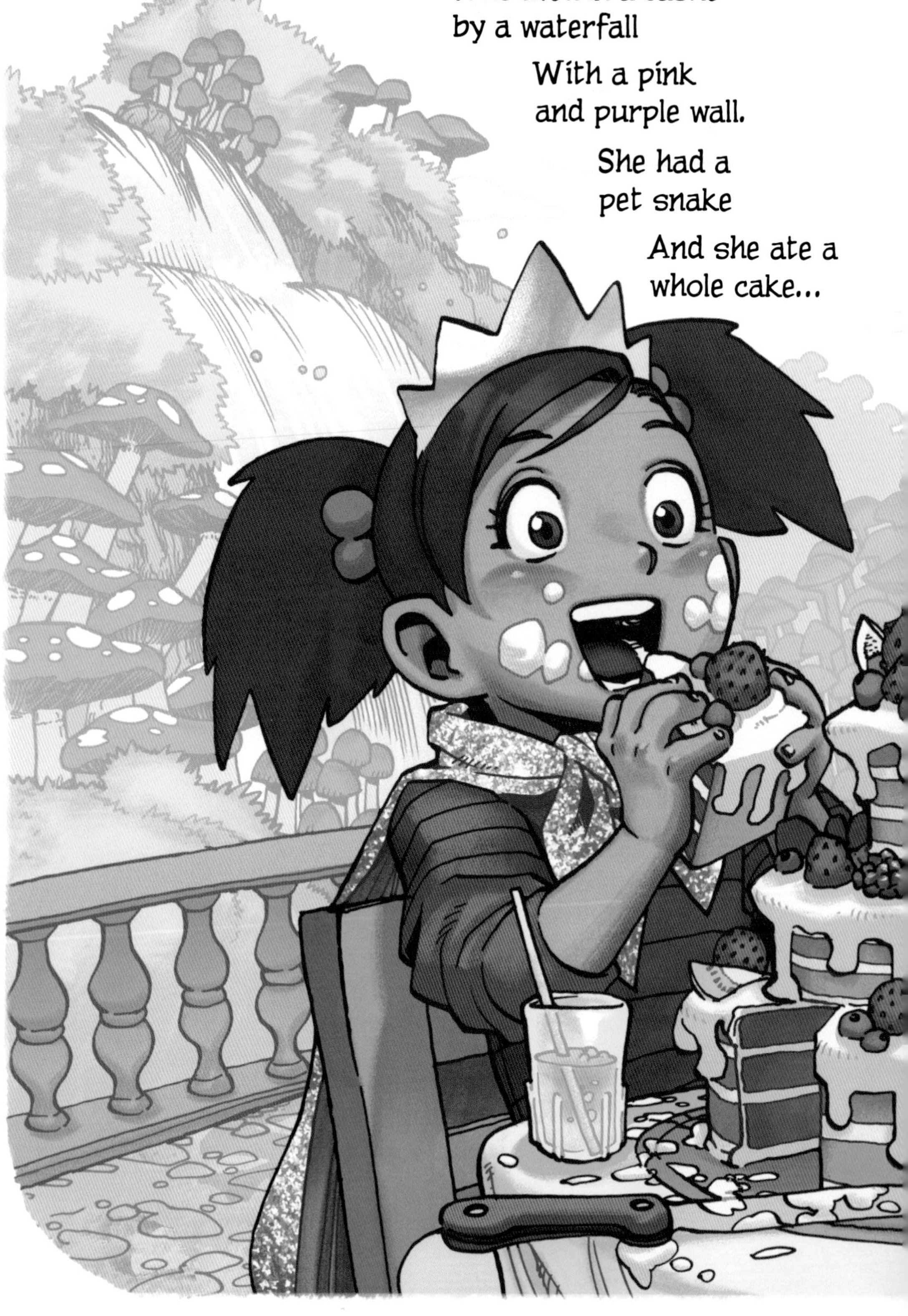

...because there wasn't anybody there to tell her what to do.

So she did what she wanted to...

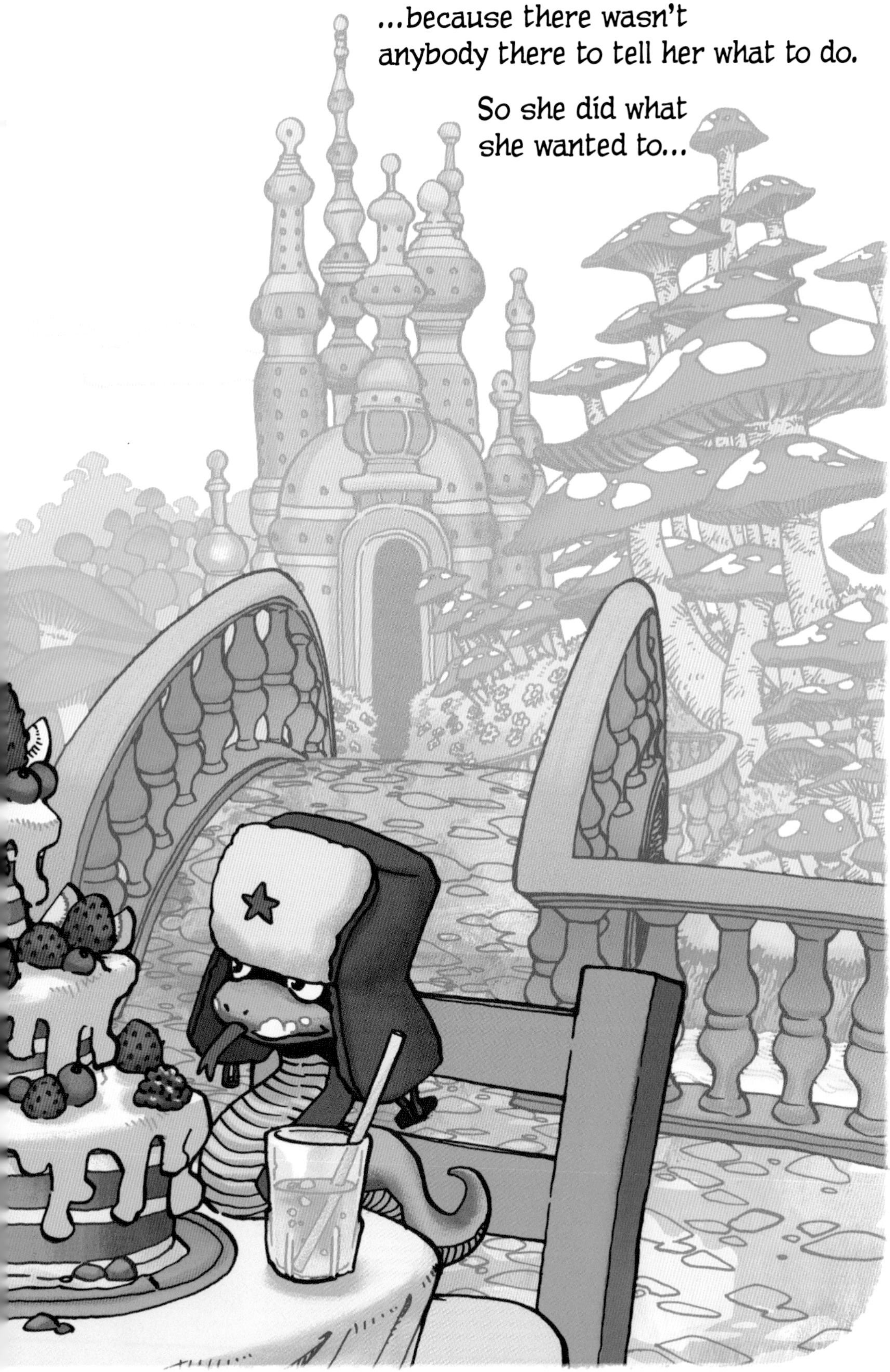

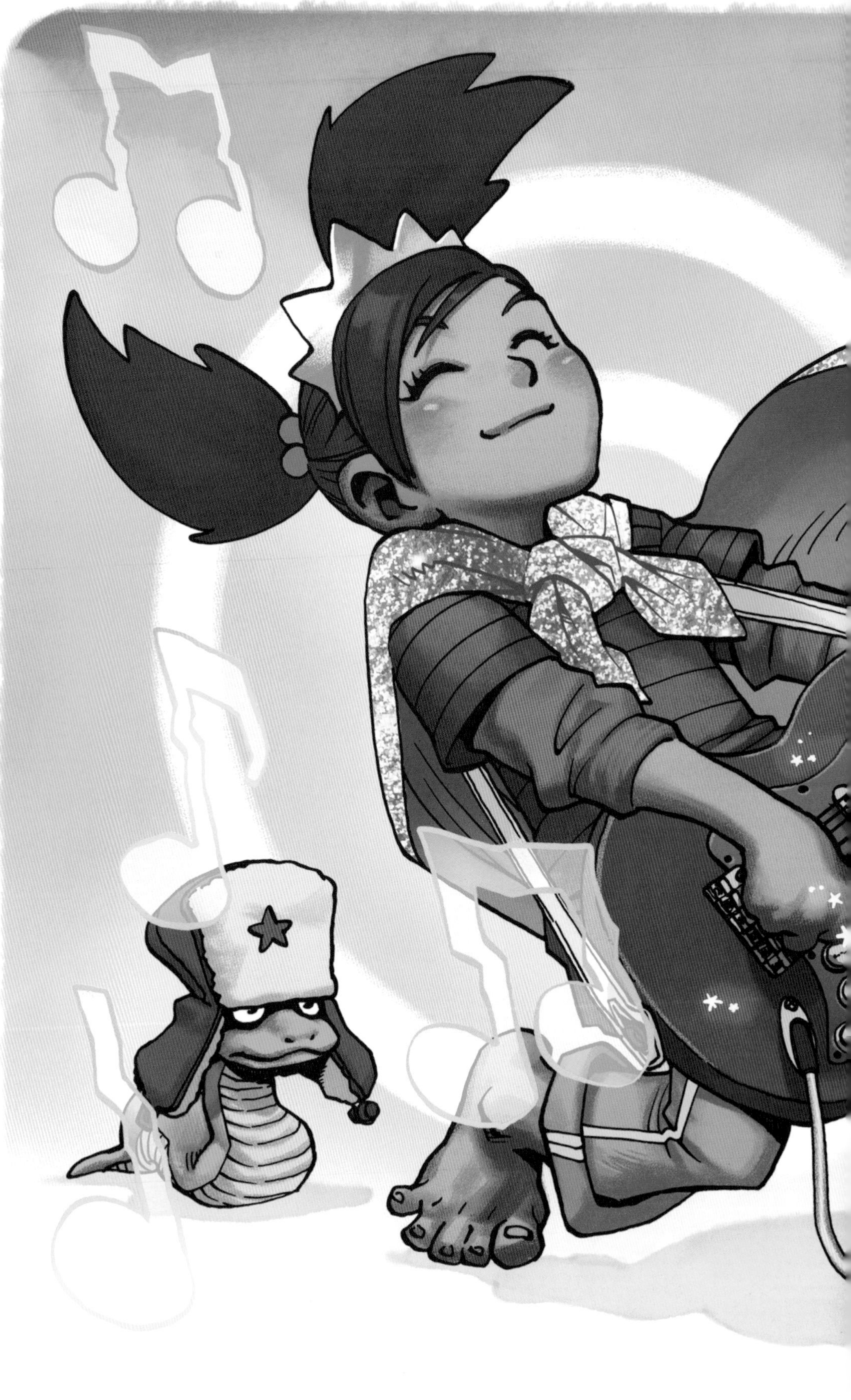

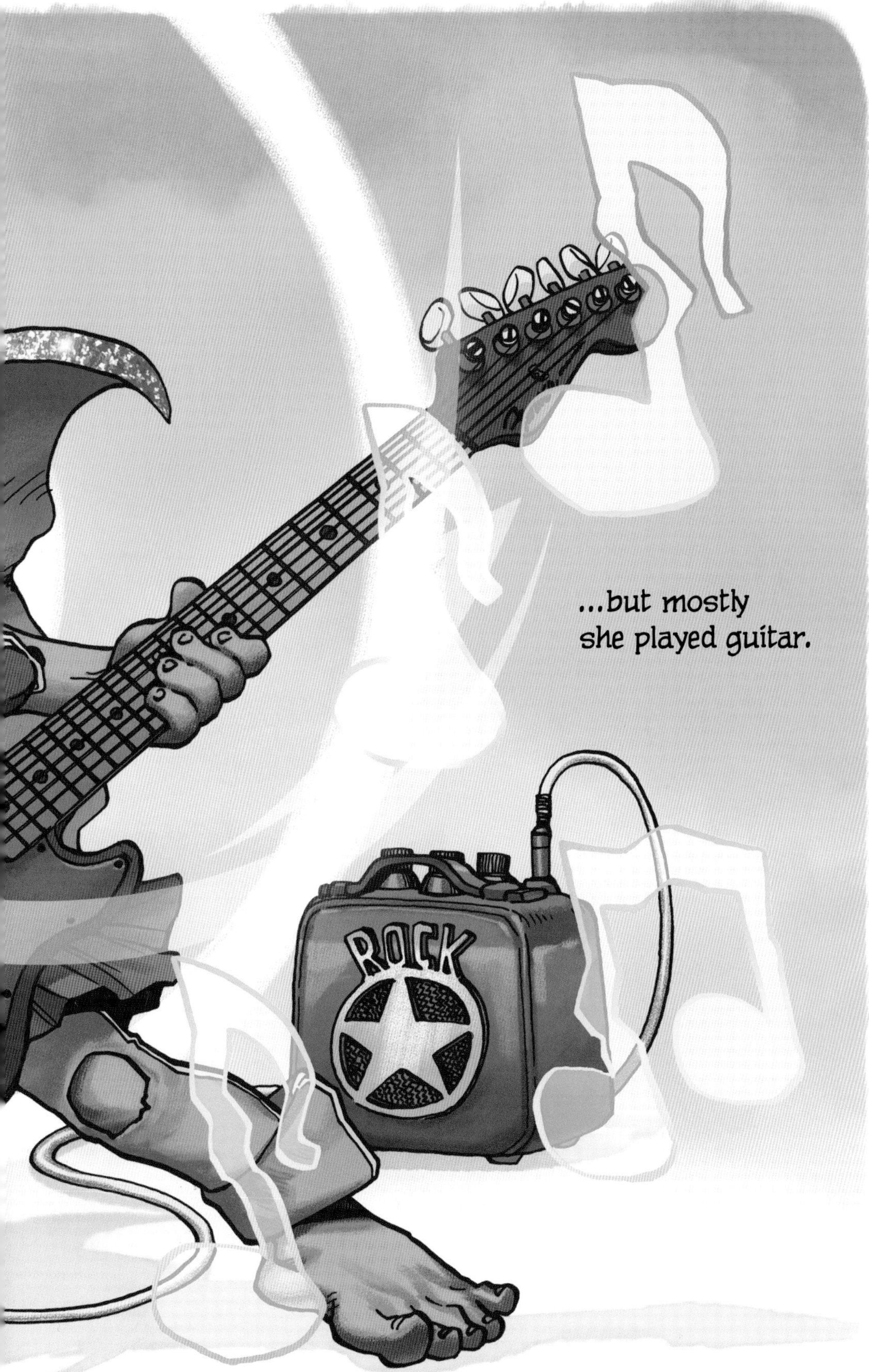
ROCK

...but mostly
she played guitar.

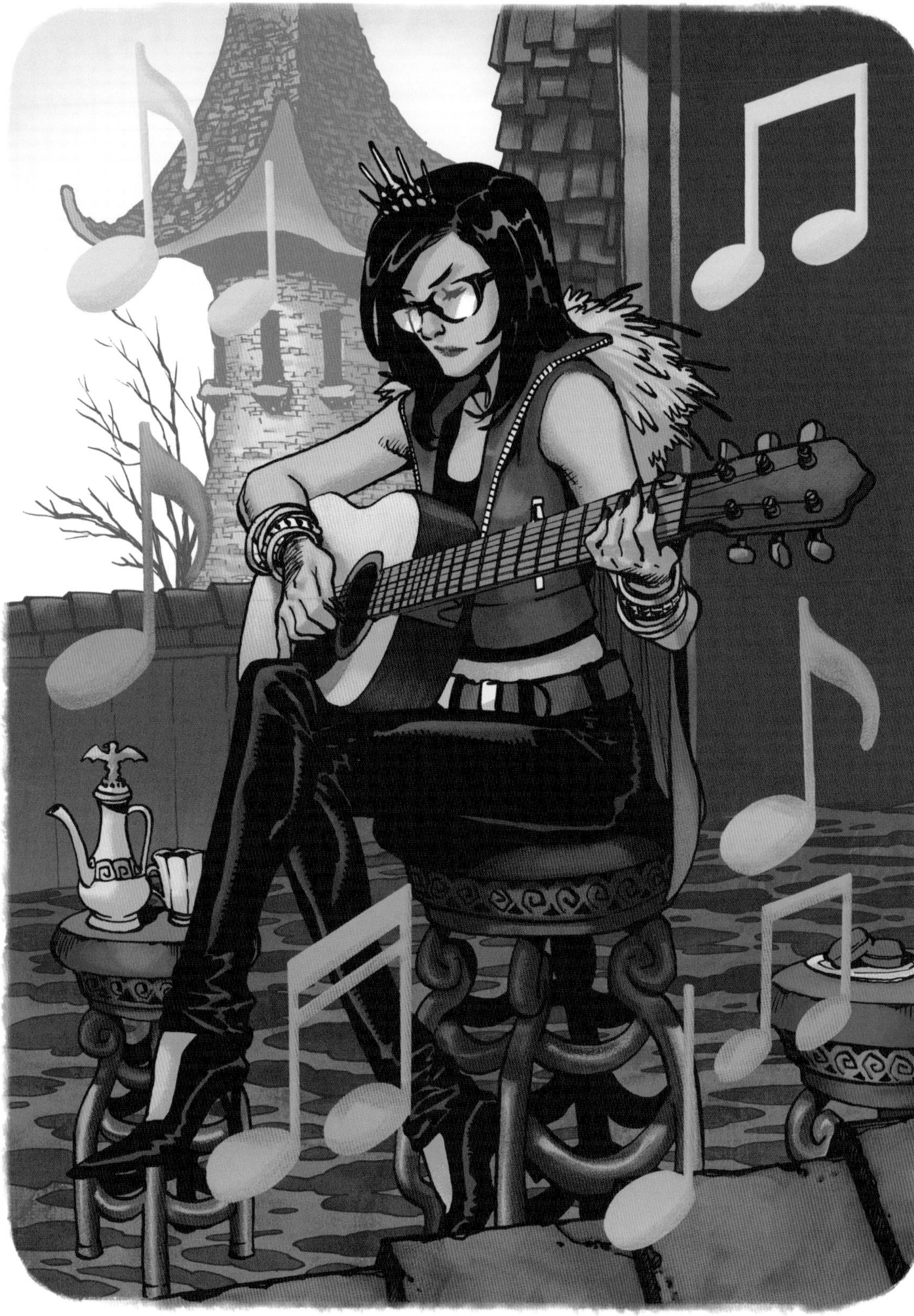

So did the very wicked queen
Who lived a mile down the stream

And who nearly lost her mind
Every time she heard the grind
Of the princess's red guitar.

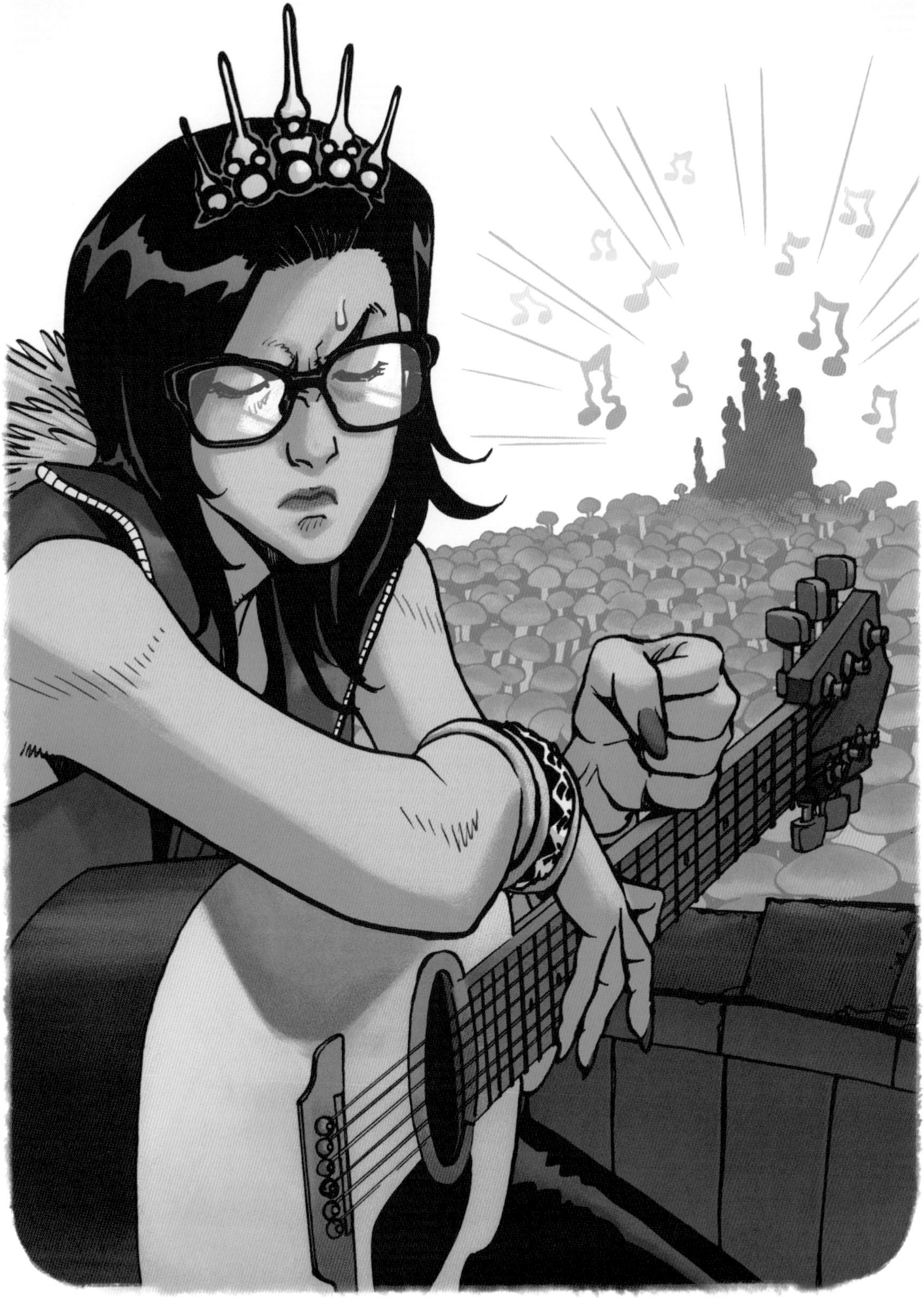

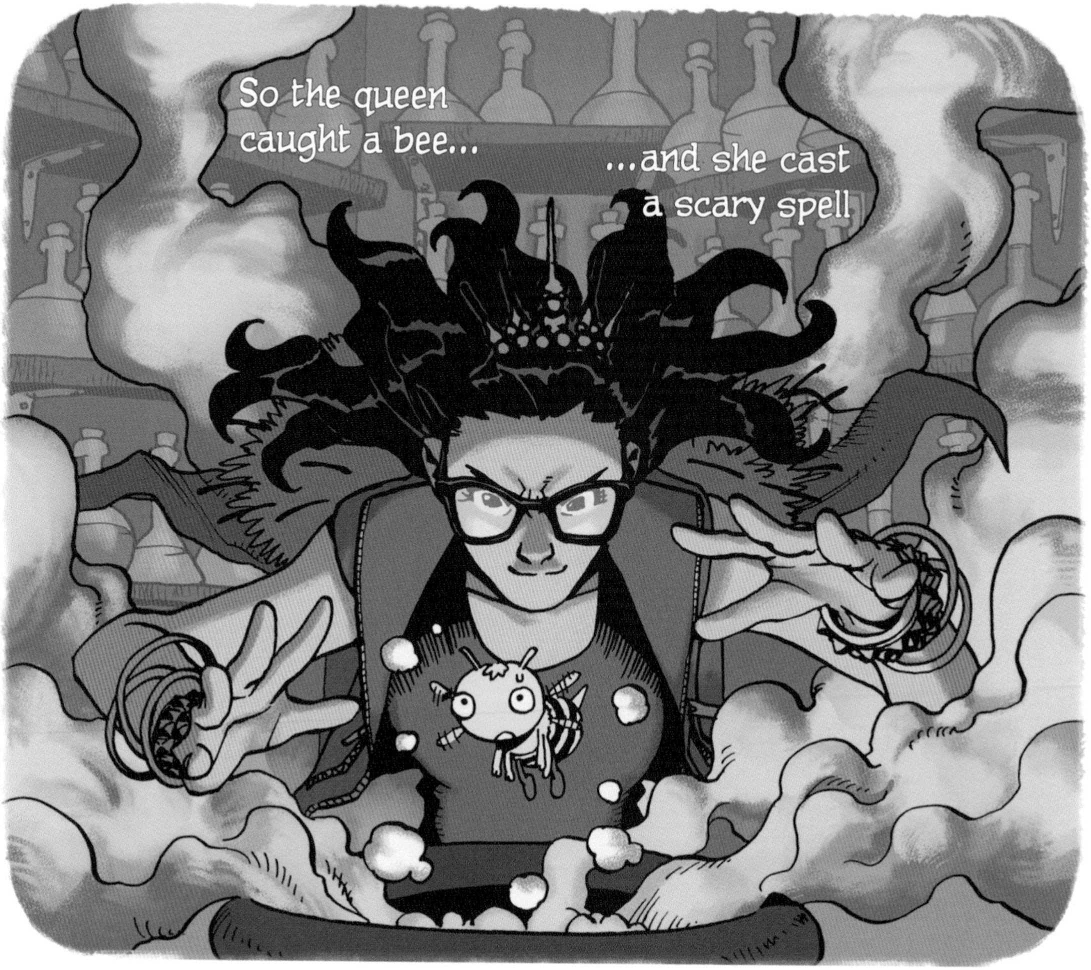
So the queen caught a bee...
...and she cast a scary spell

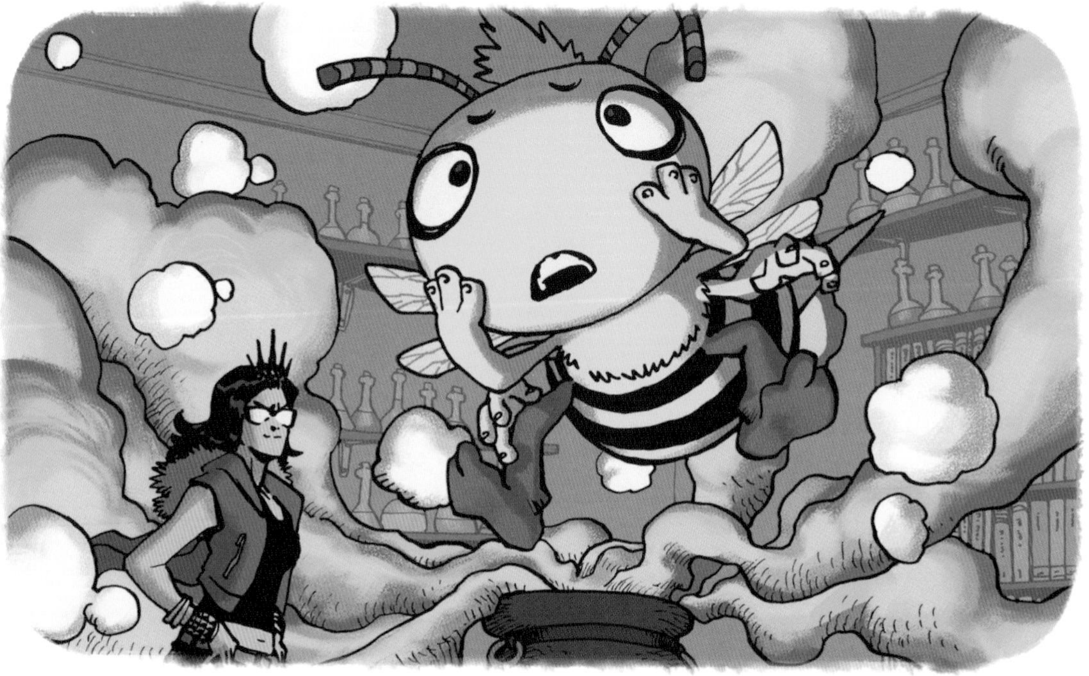

And the bee grew twelve times bigger and let off a stinky smell!

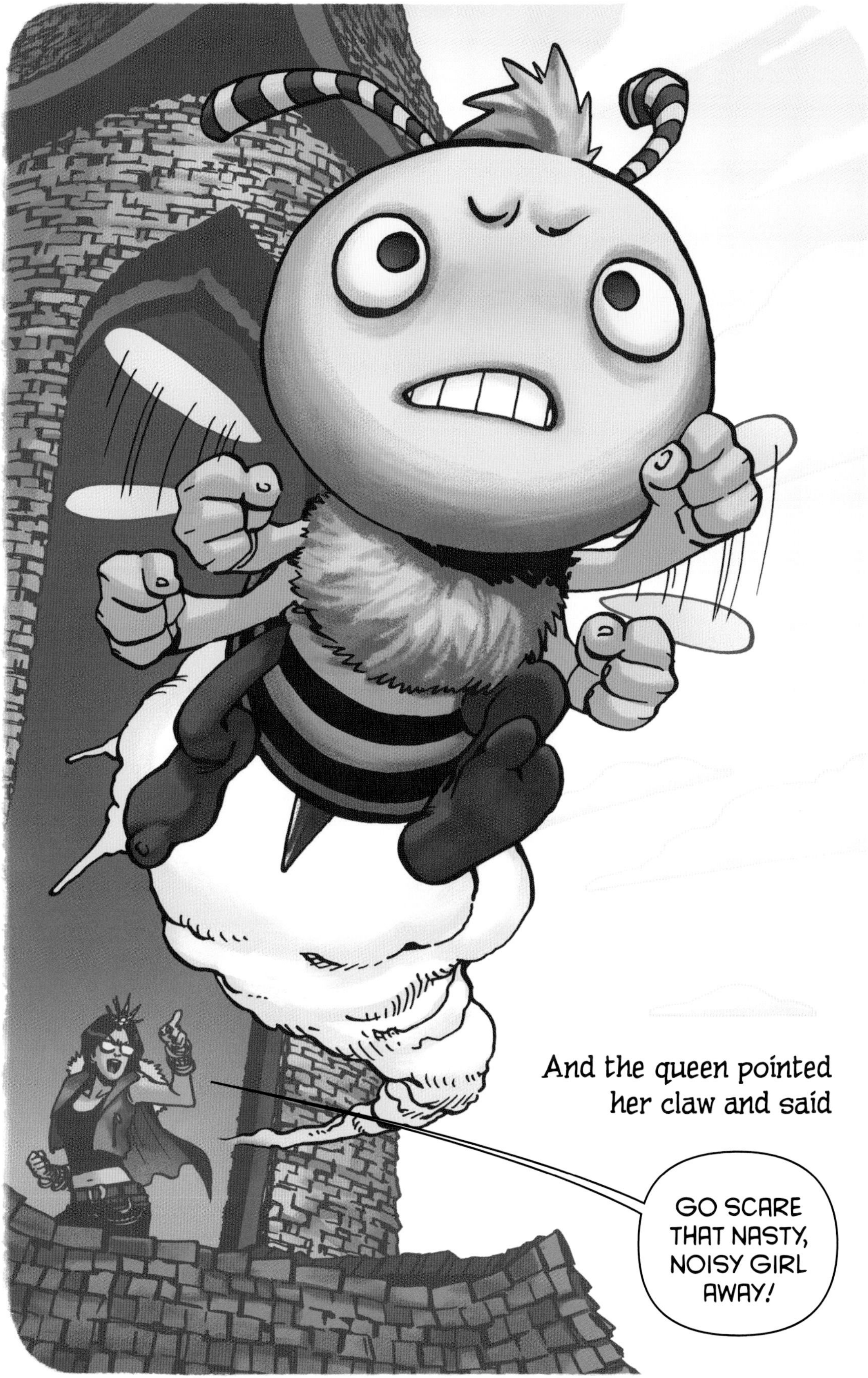
And the queen pointed
her claw and said
GO SCARE THAT NASTY, NOISY GIRL AWAY!

But the princess
loved all bugs!
So she just gave
it lots of hugs

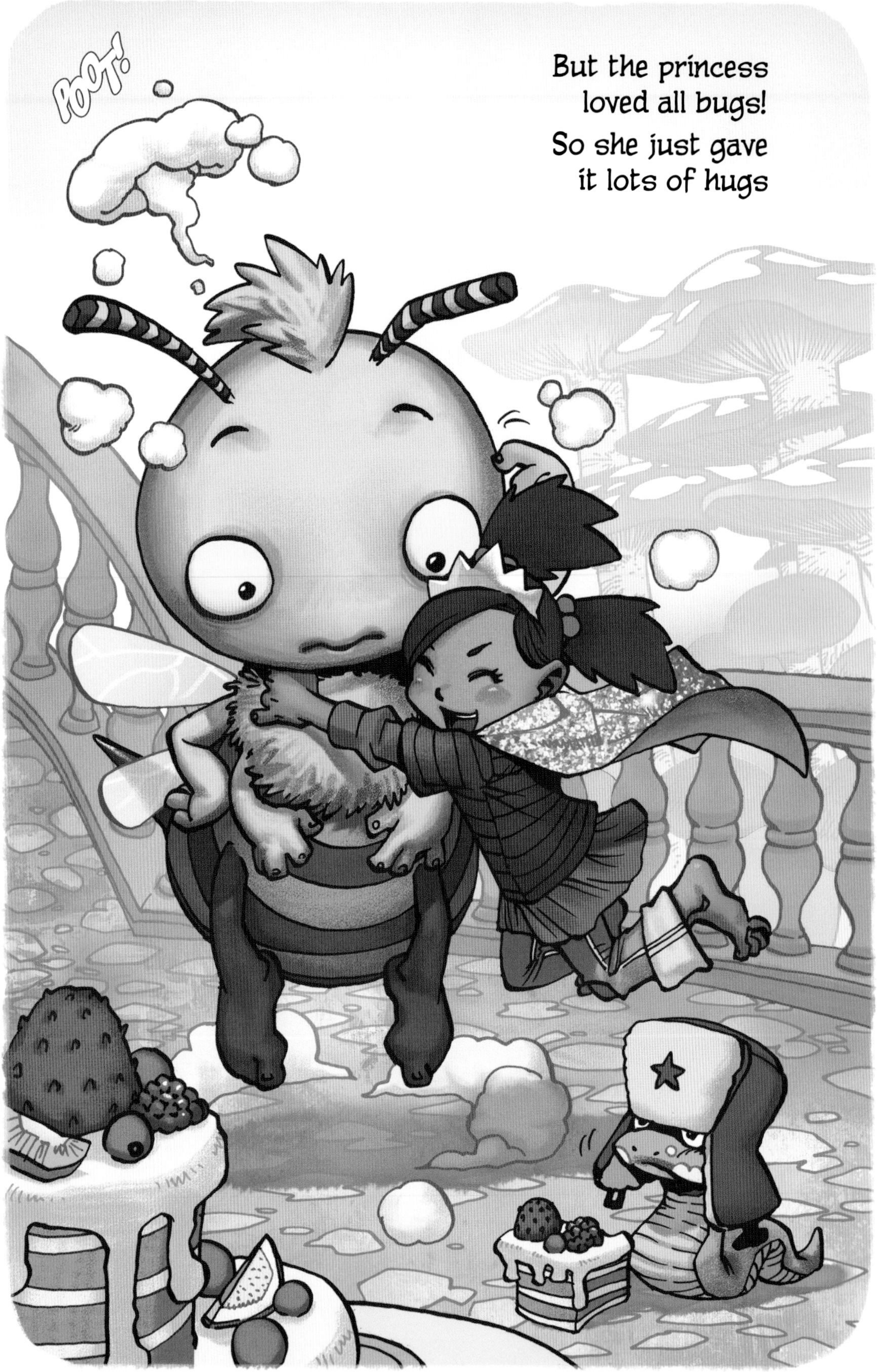
POOT!

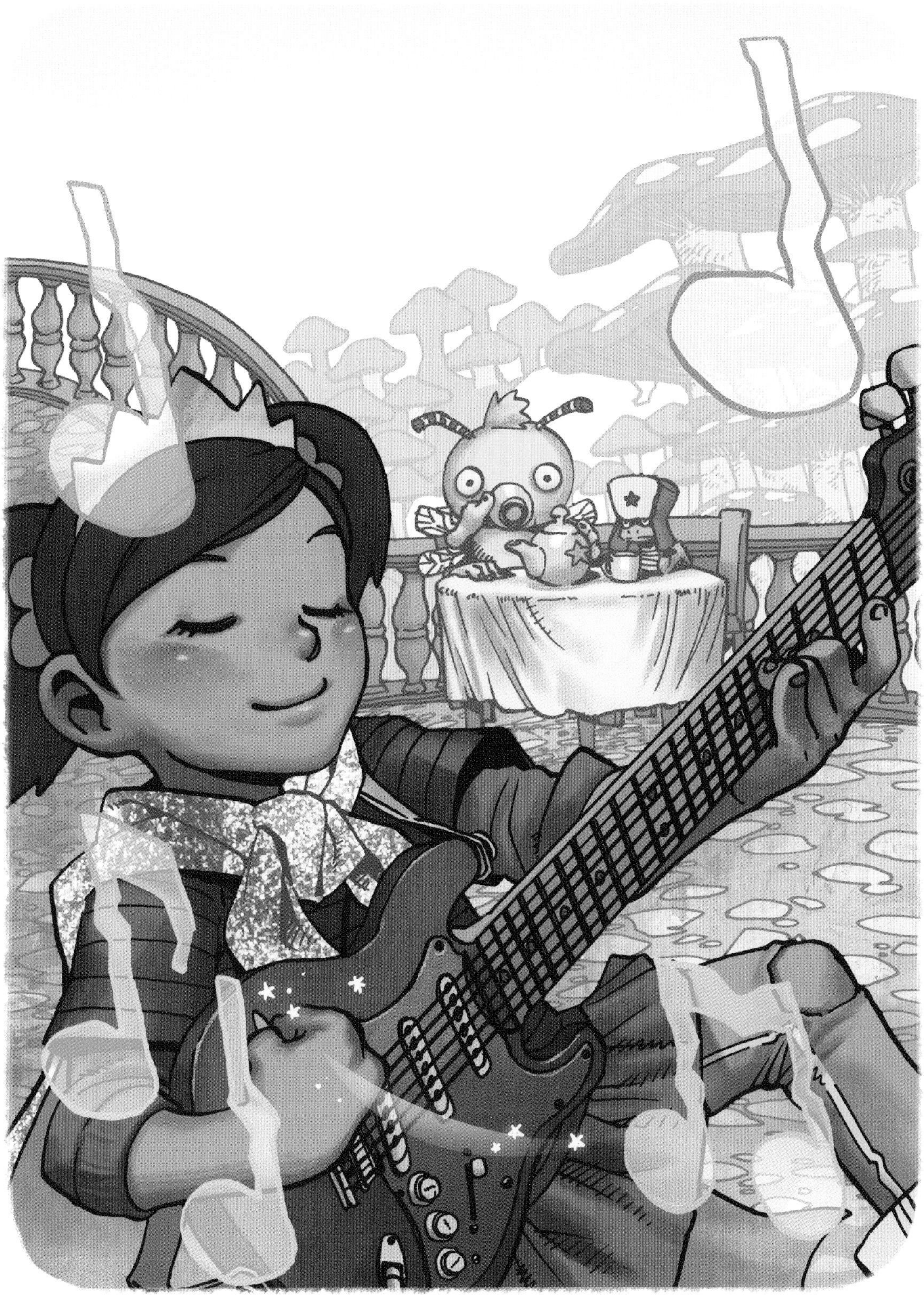

And invited it to tea and music time.

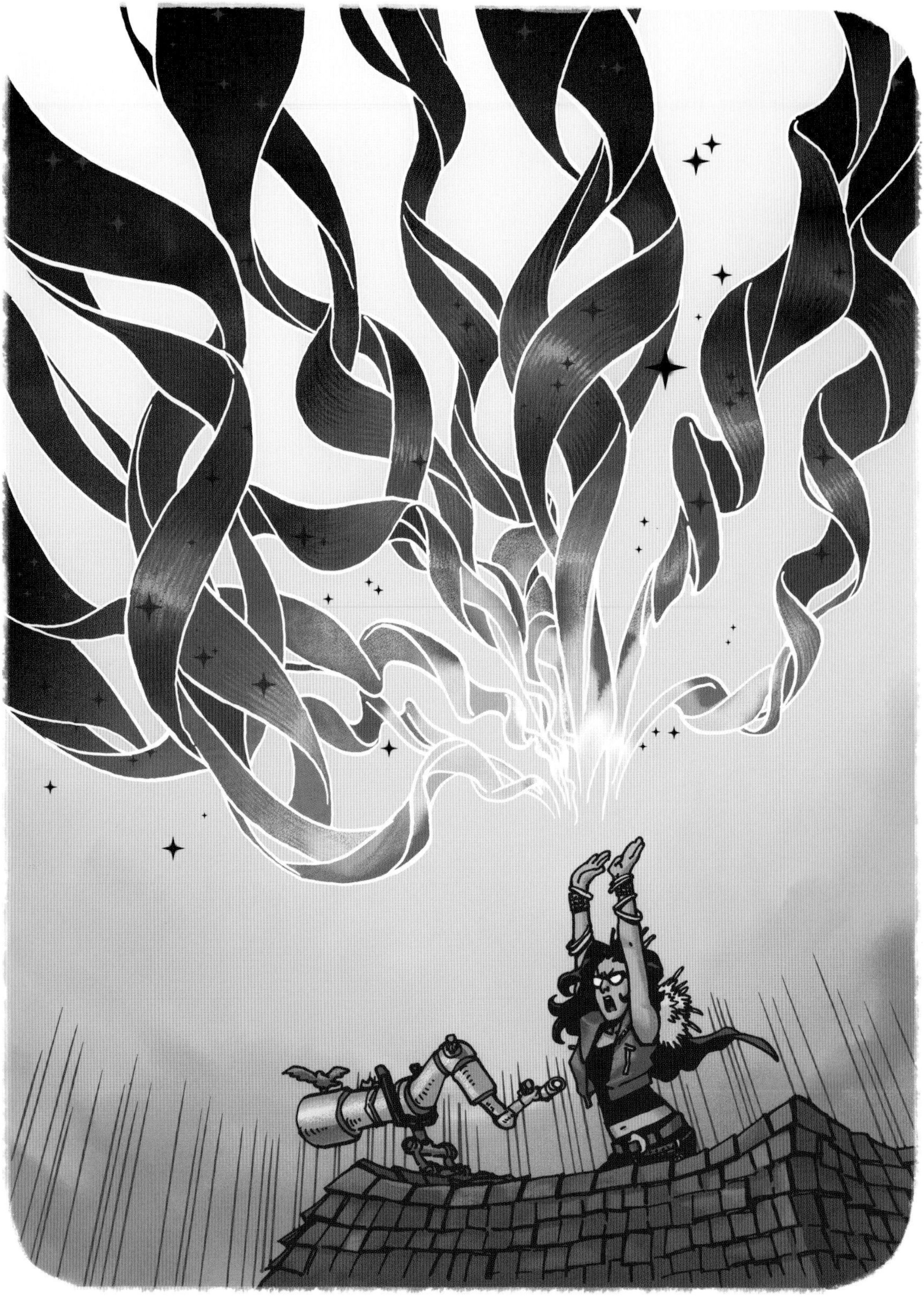

So the witch banished the sun!

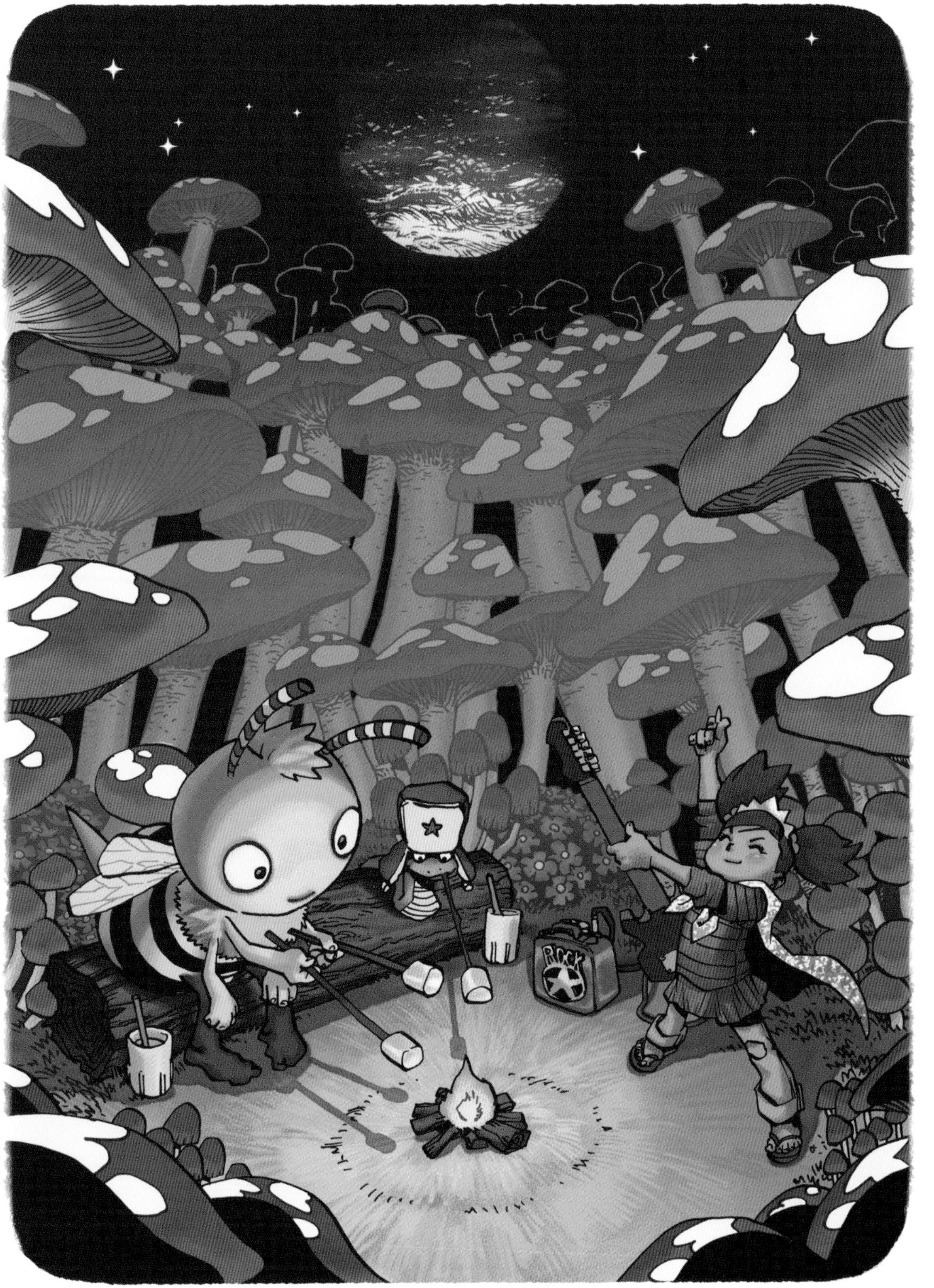
ROCK

But the princess just had fun
With a campout, lots of marshmallows and friends.

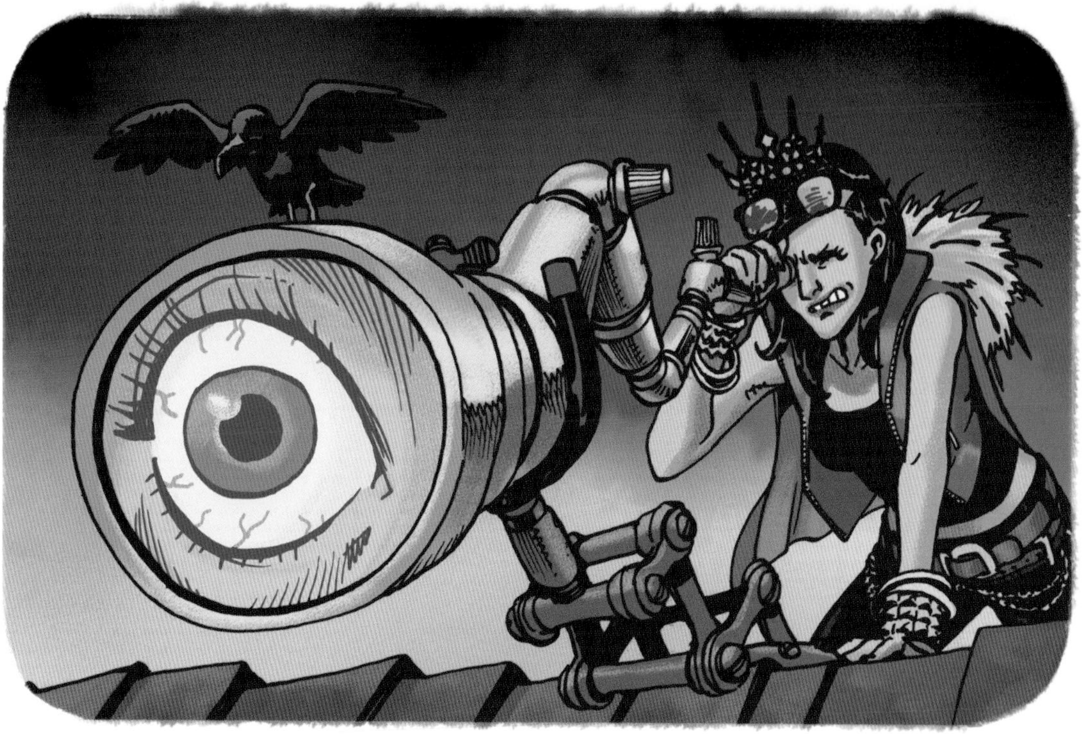

The witch got quite irate.
(And in truth, it was quite late.)

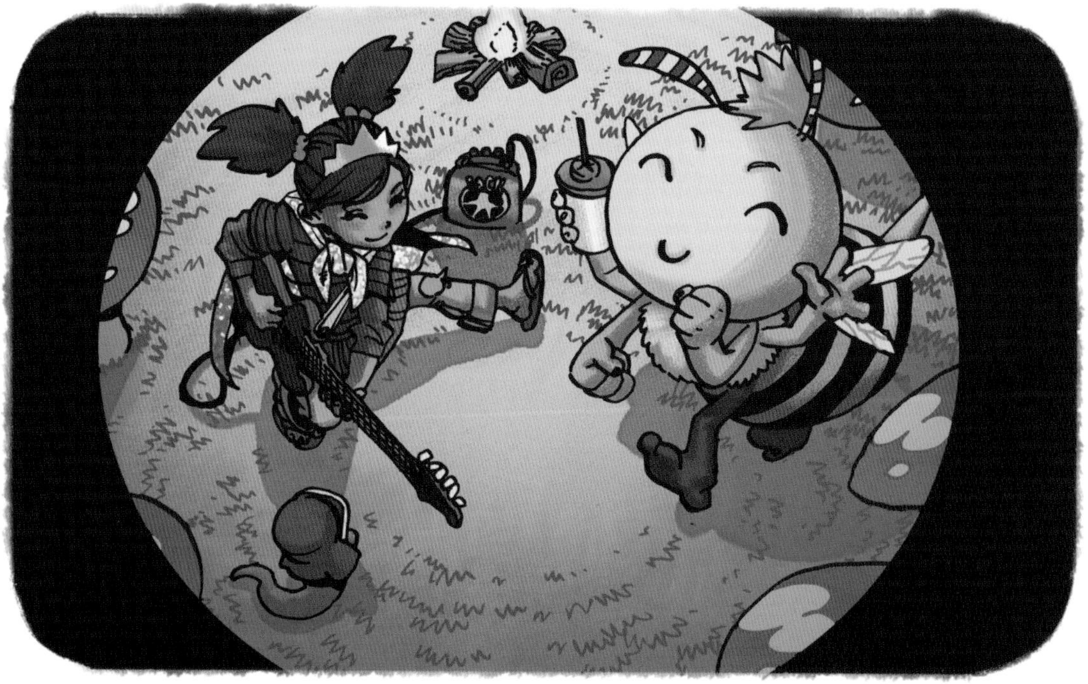

And the princess kept on playing
with the clanging and the jangling

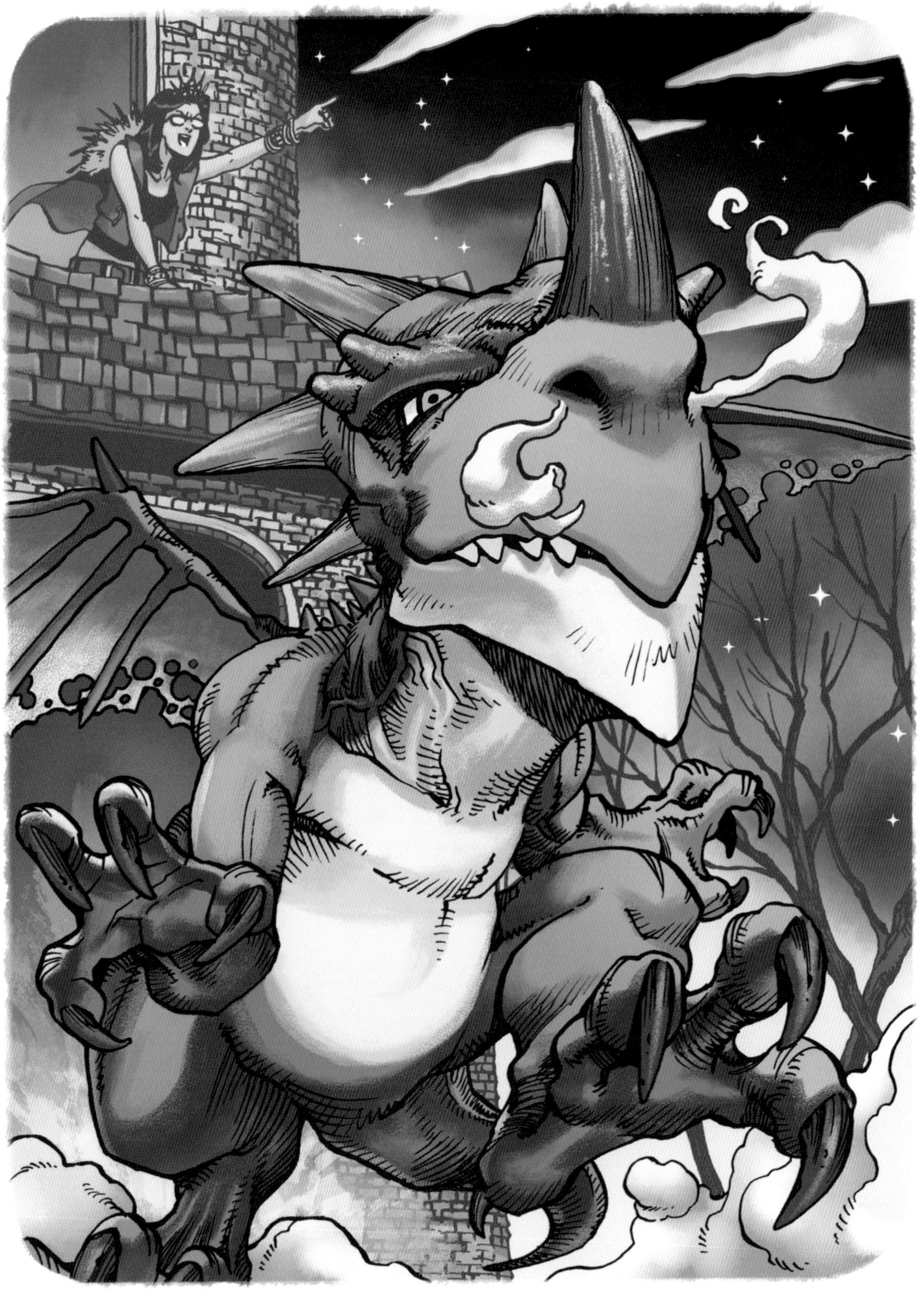

So the witch sent her blue dragon to
steal and burn poor Glory's red guitar!

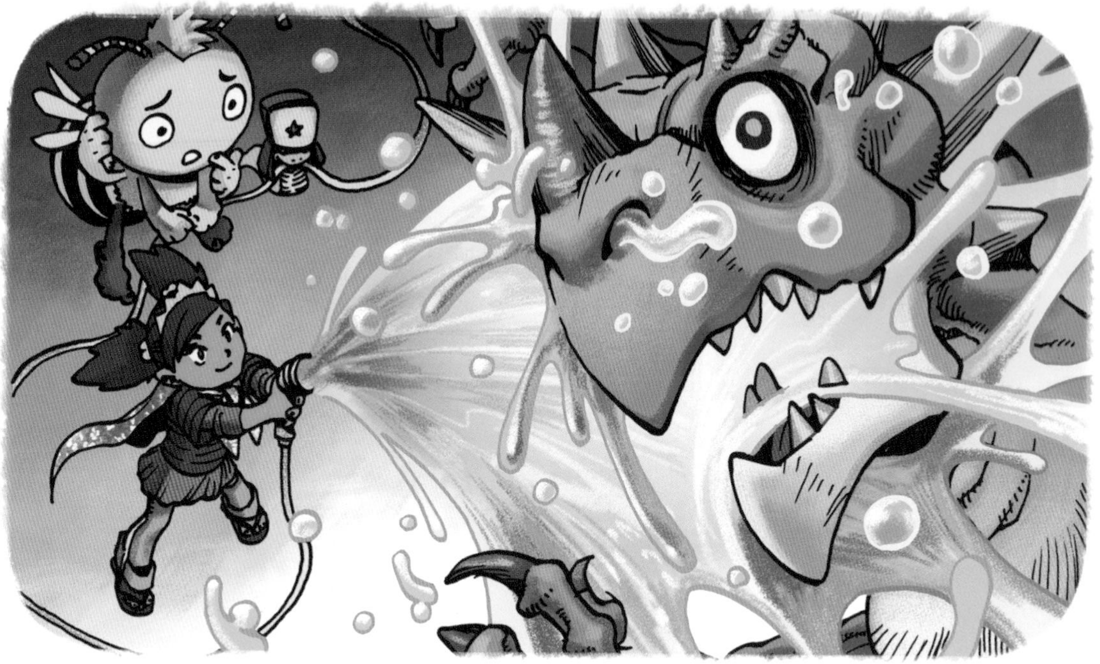

But Glory turned on the garden hose
And she got him in the nose!

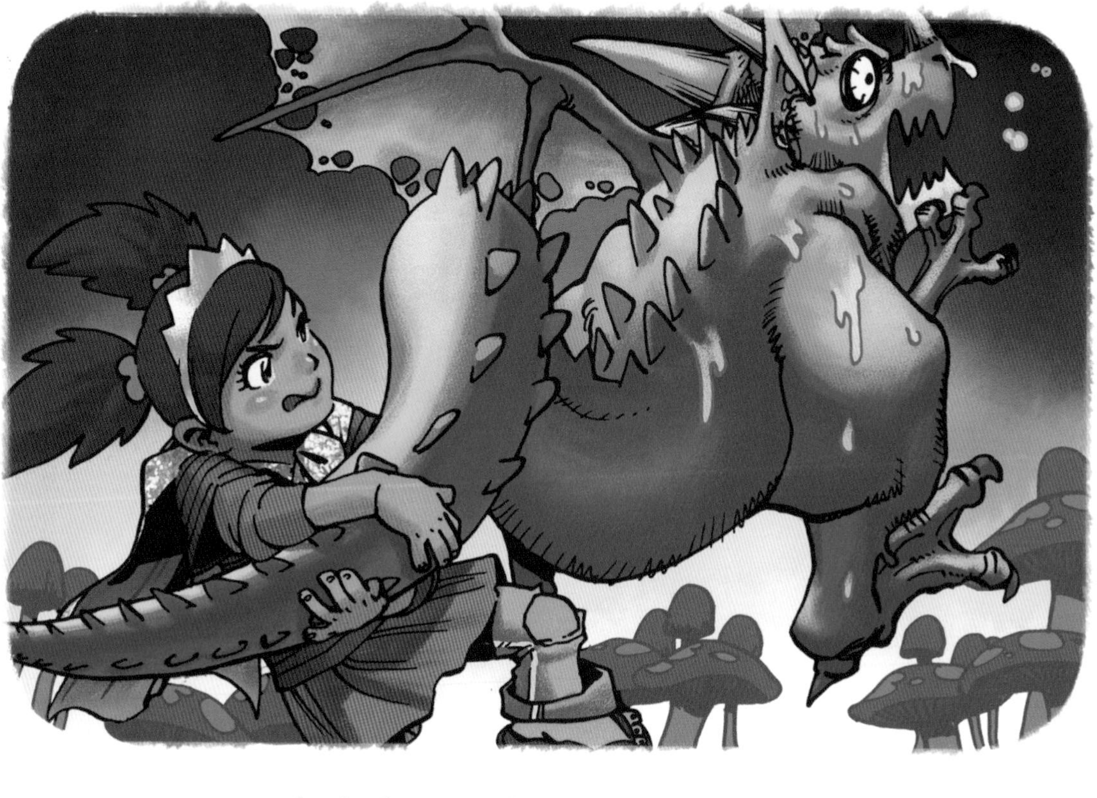

And she caught him by the tail!
And ignored his mighty wail!

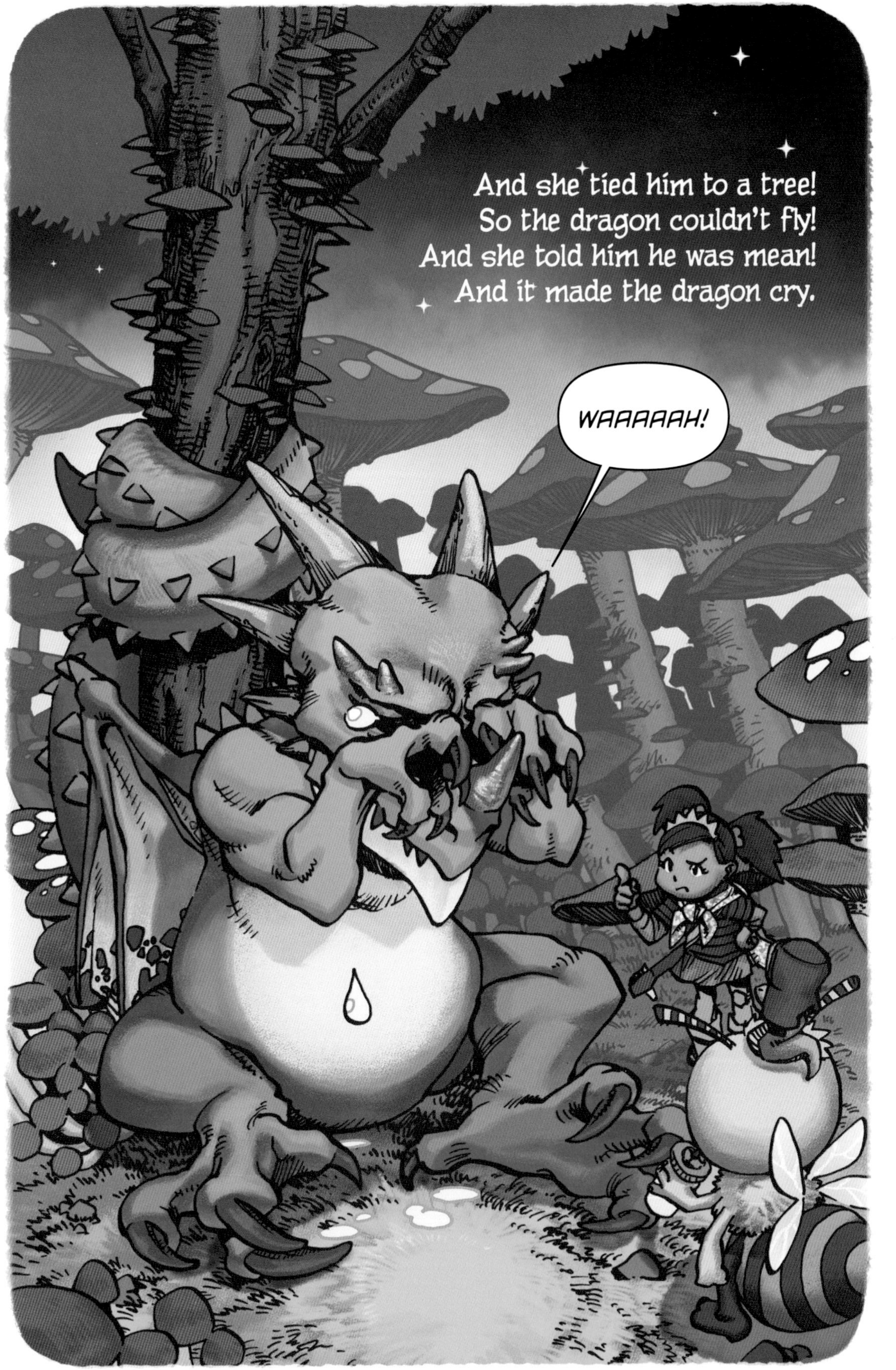
And she tied him to a tree!
So the dragon couldn't fly!
And she told him he was mean!
And it made the dragon cry.
WAAAAAAH!

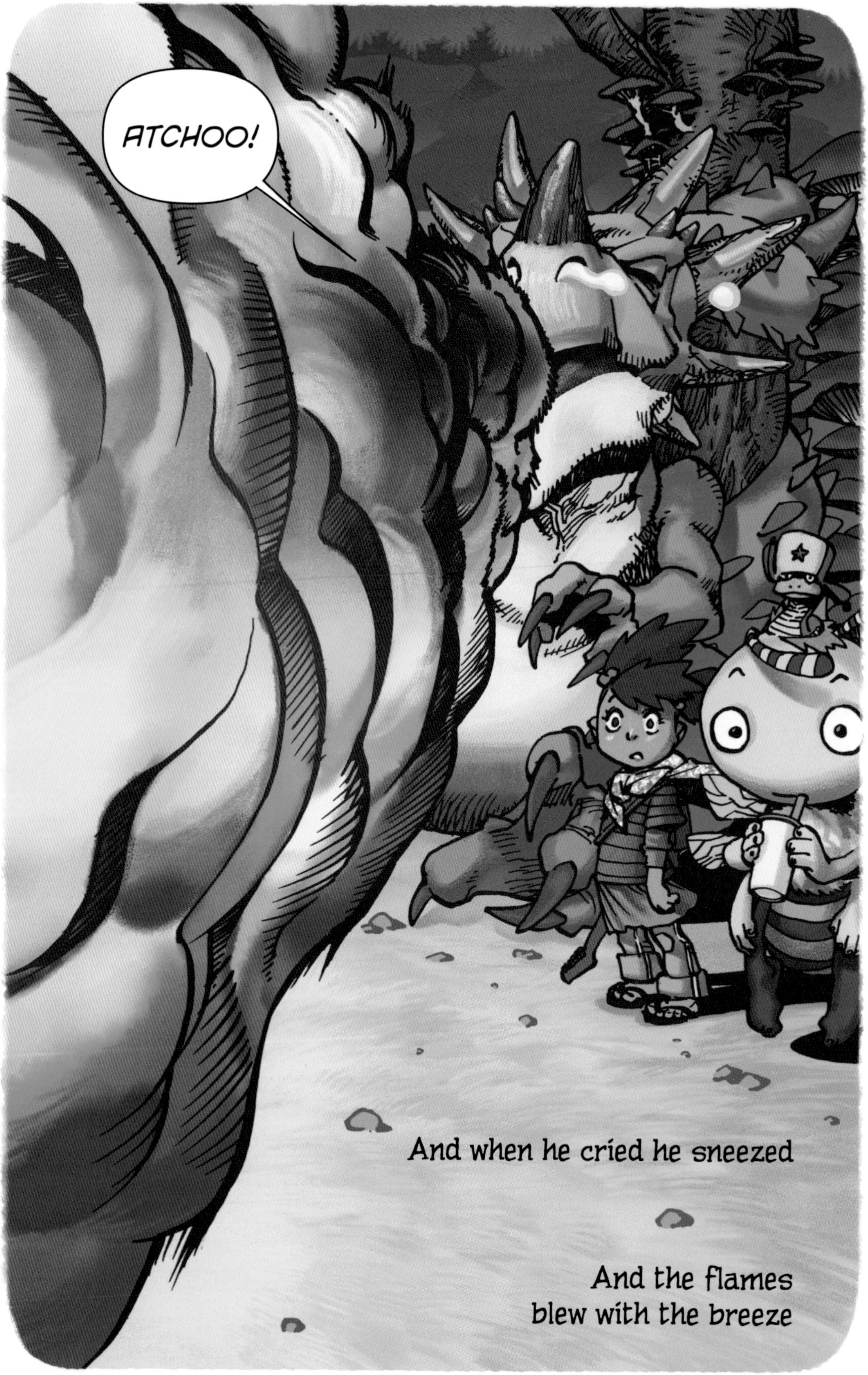
ATCHOO!
And when he cried he sneezed
And the flames
blew with the breeze

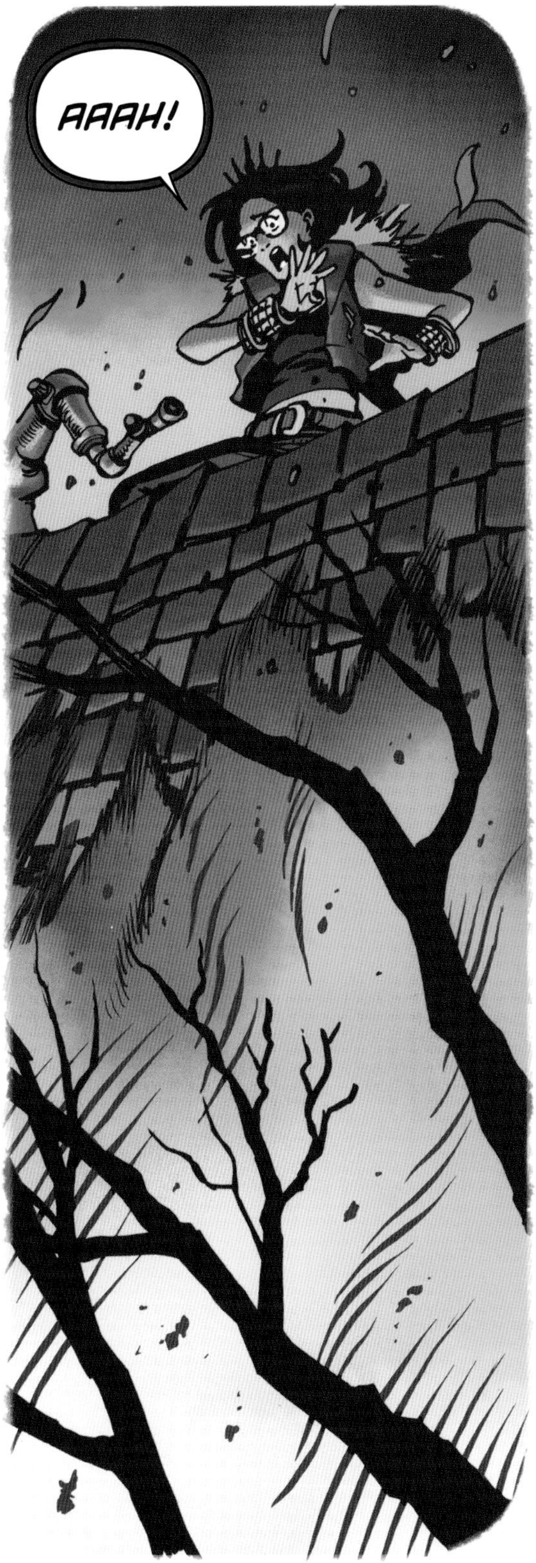
AAAH!

And the witch's
forest burned

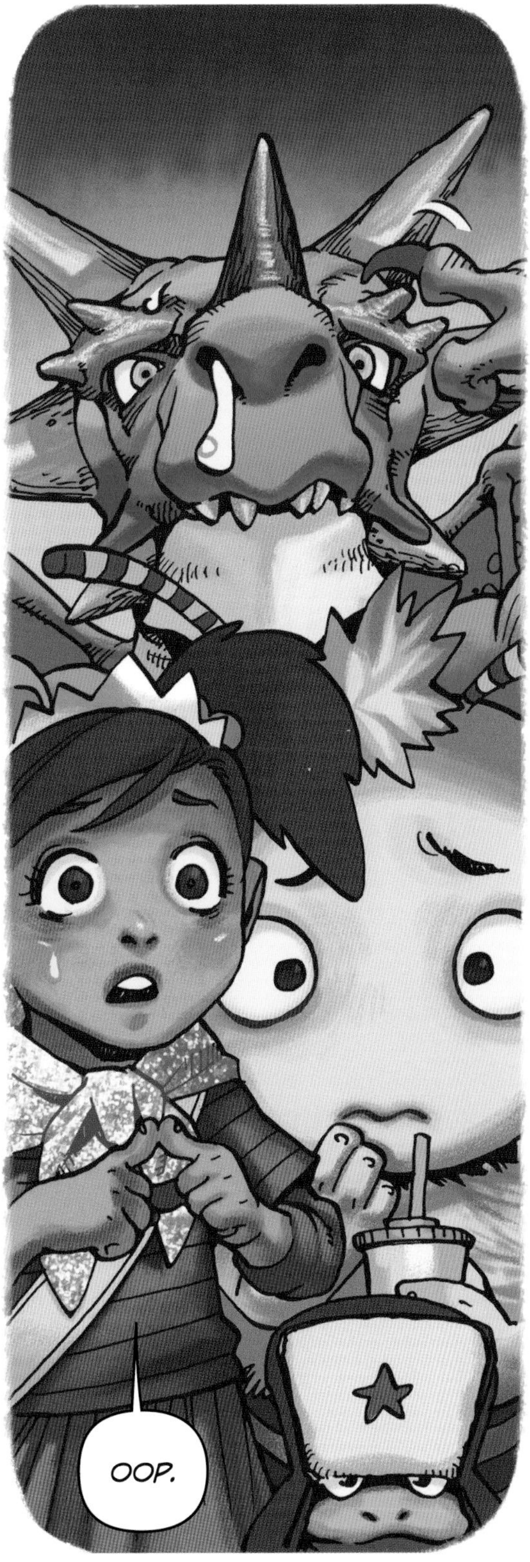
OOP.

And Glory's
stomach churned

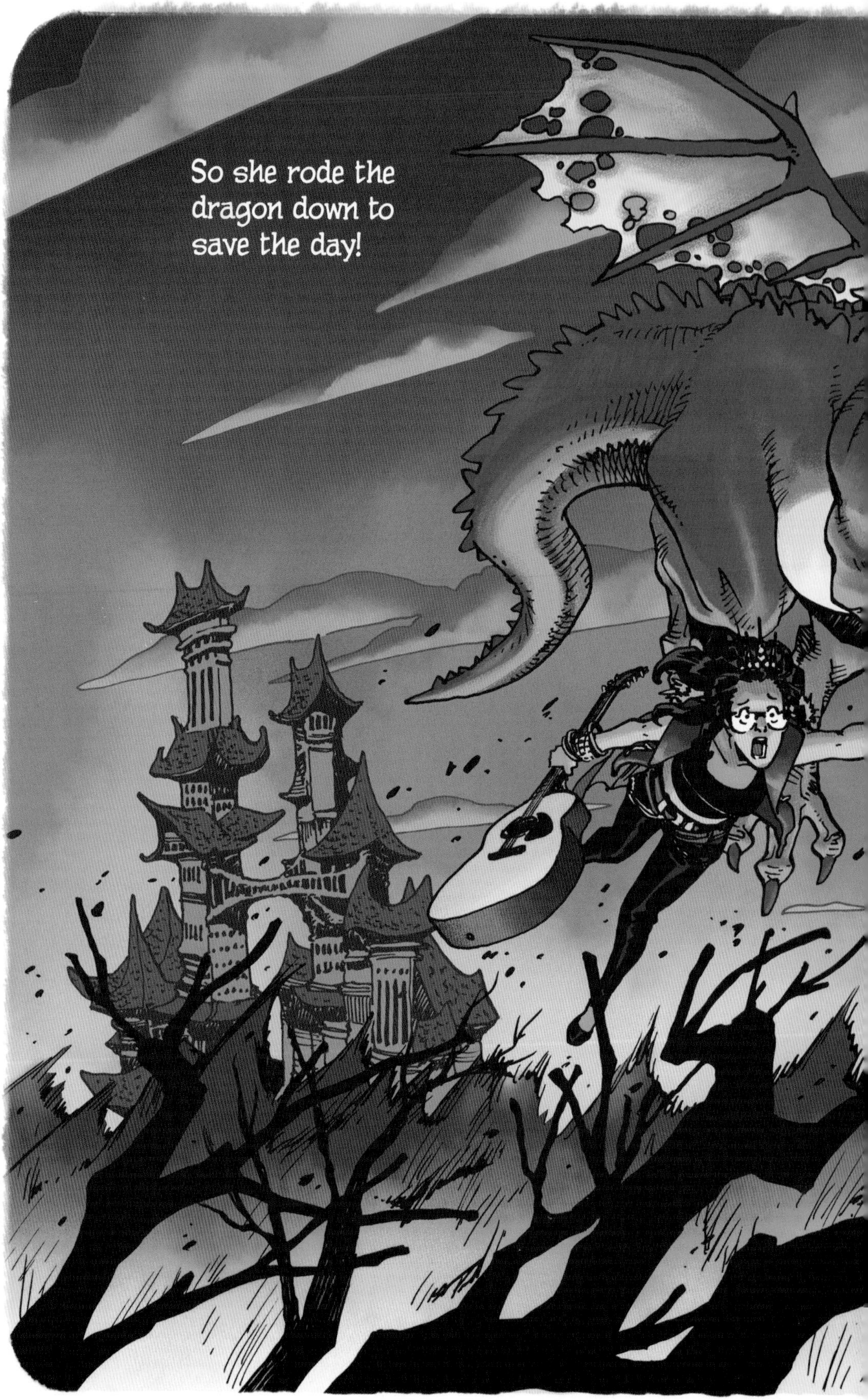
So she rode the dragon down to save the day!

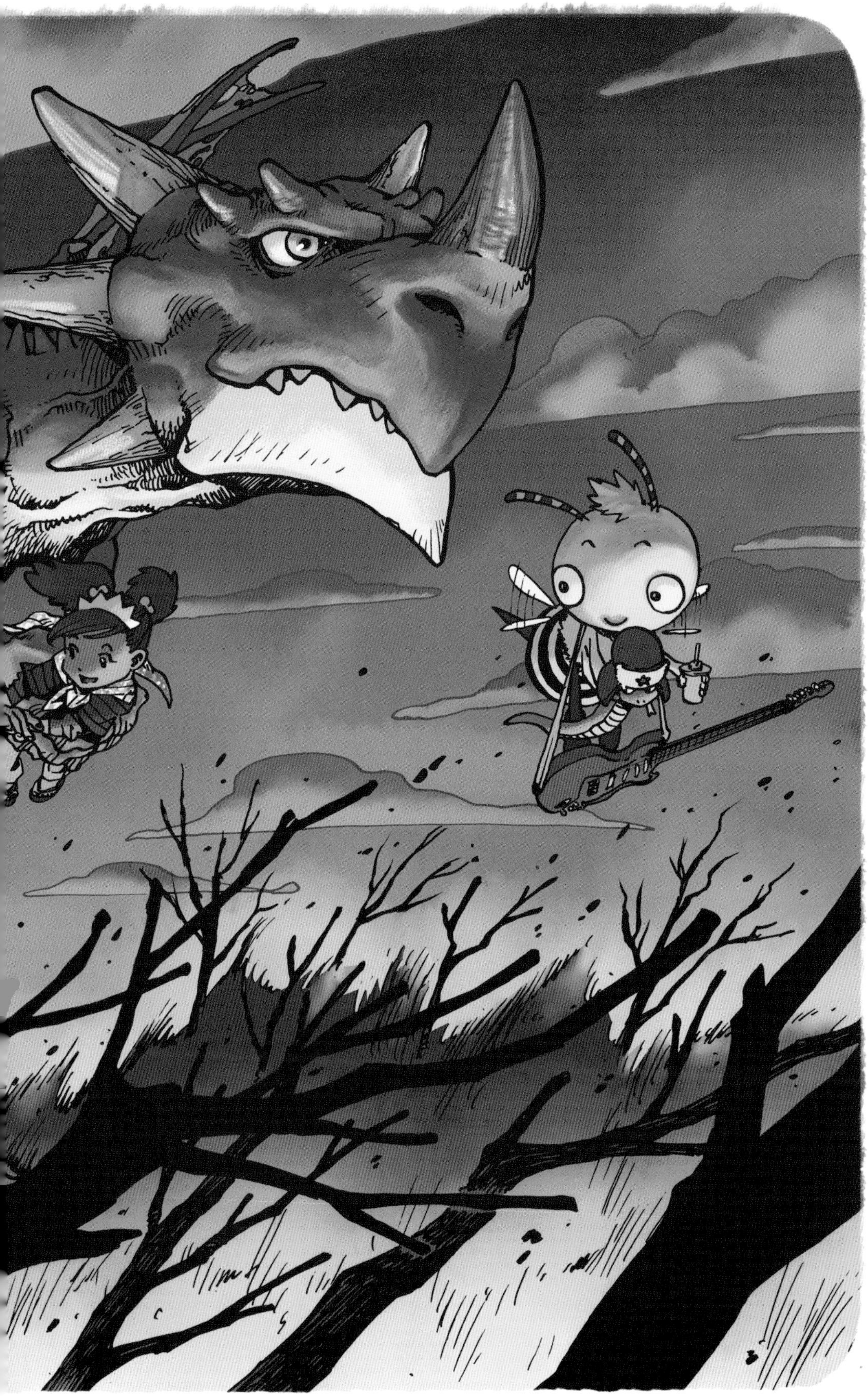

But the witch was still so angry that she called the princess

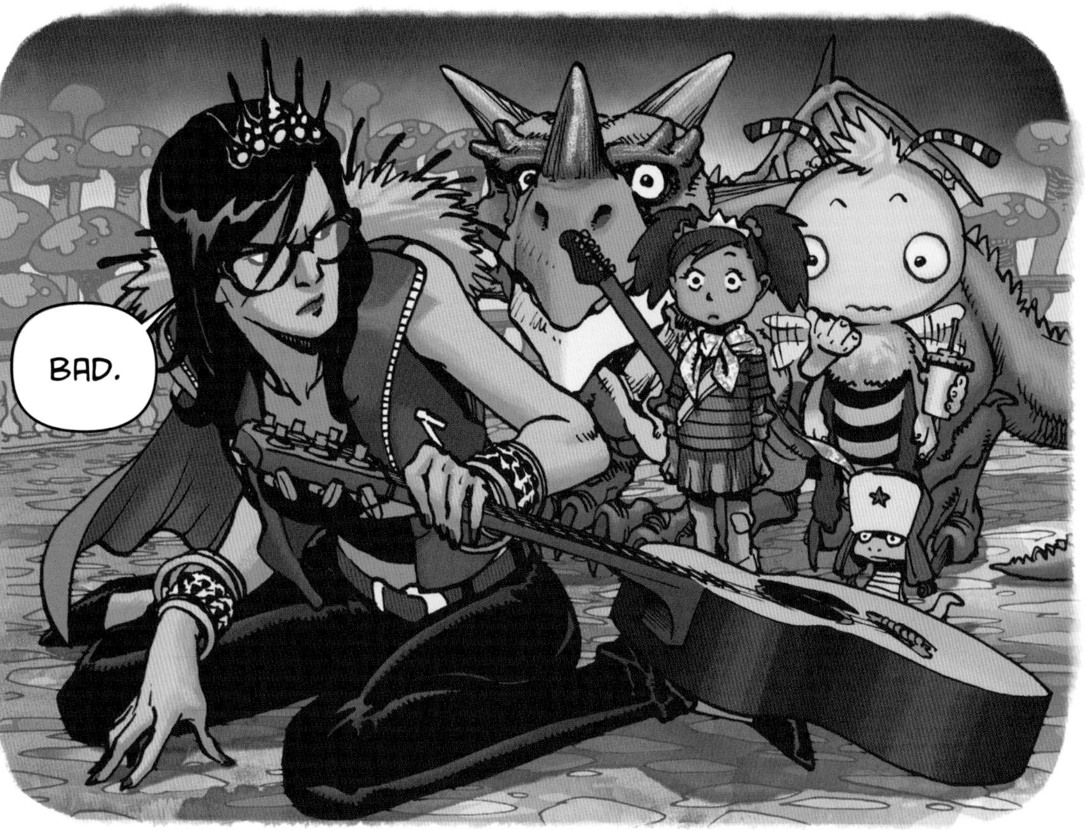
BAD.

The princess heard those mean words and they just made her

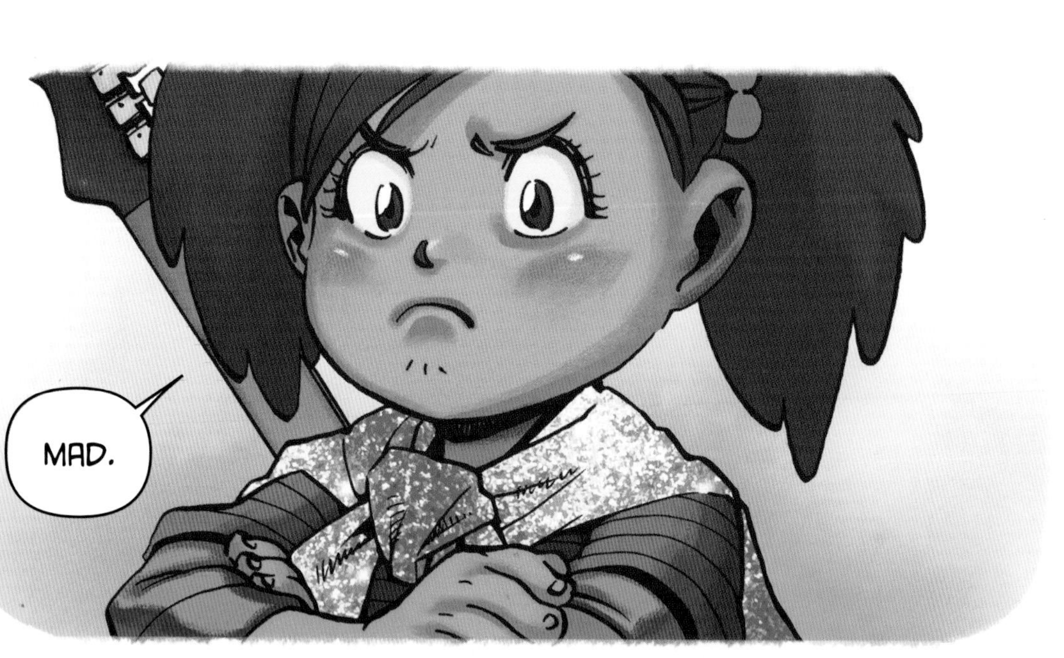
MAD.

But deep inside the witch and princess both just felt so...

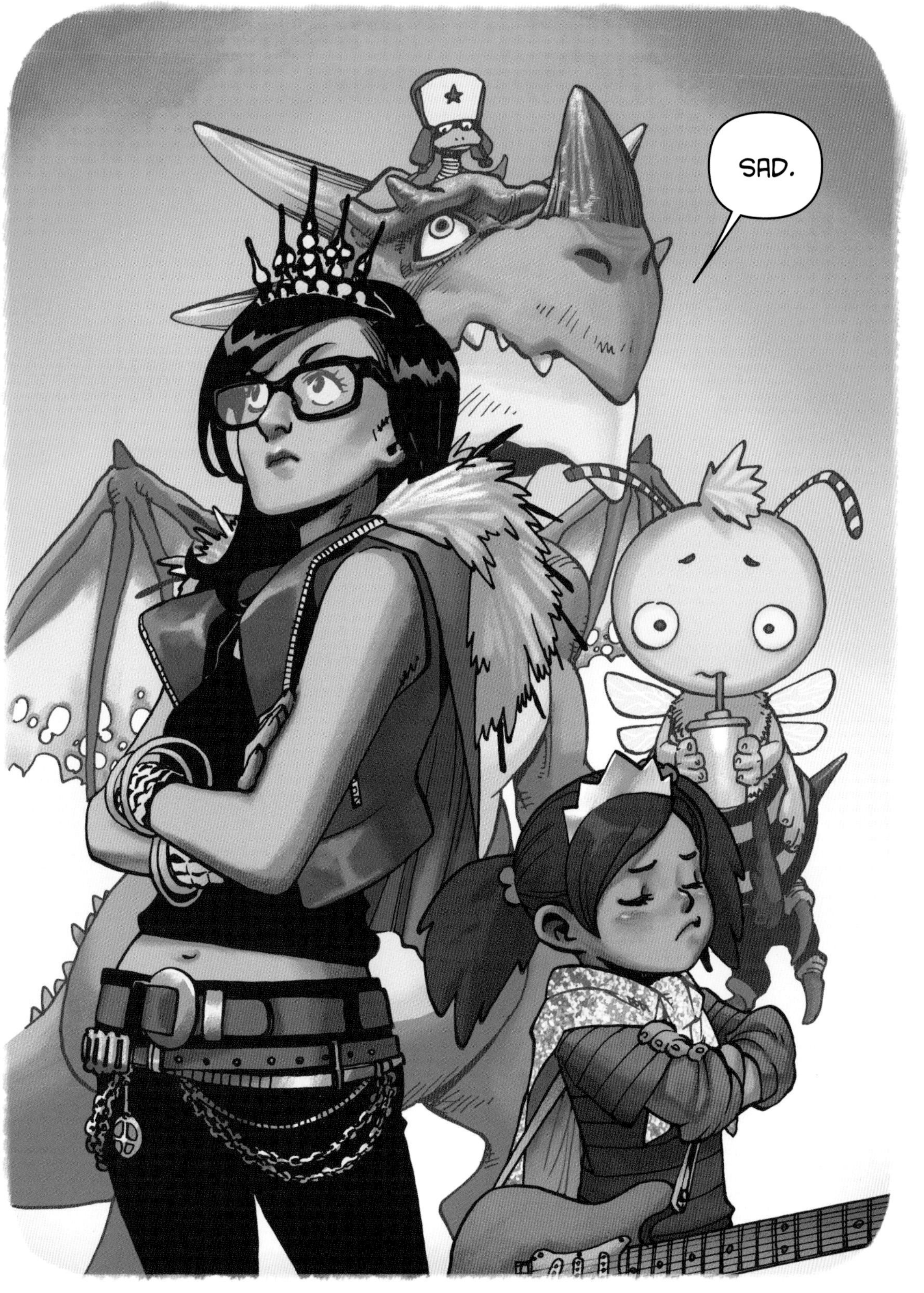
SAD.

So the princess just said

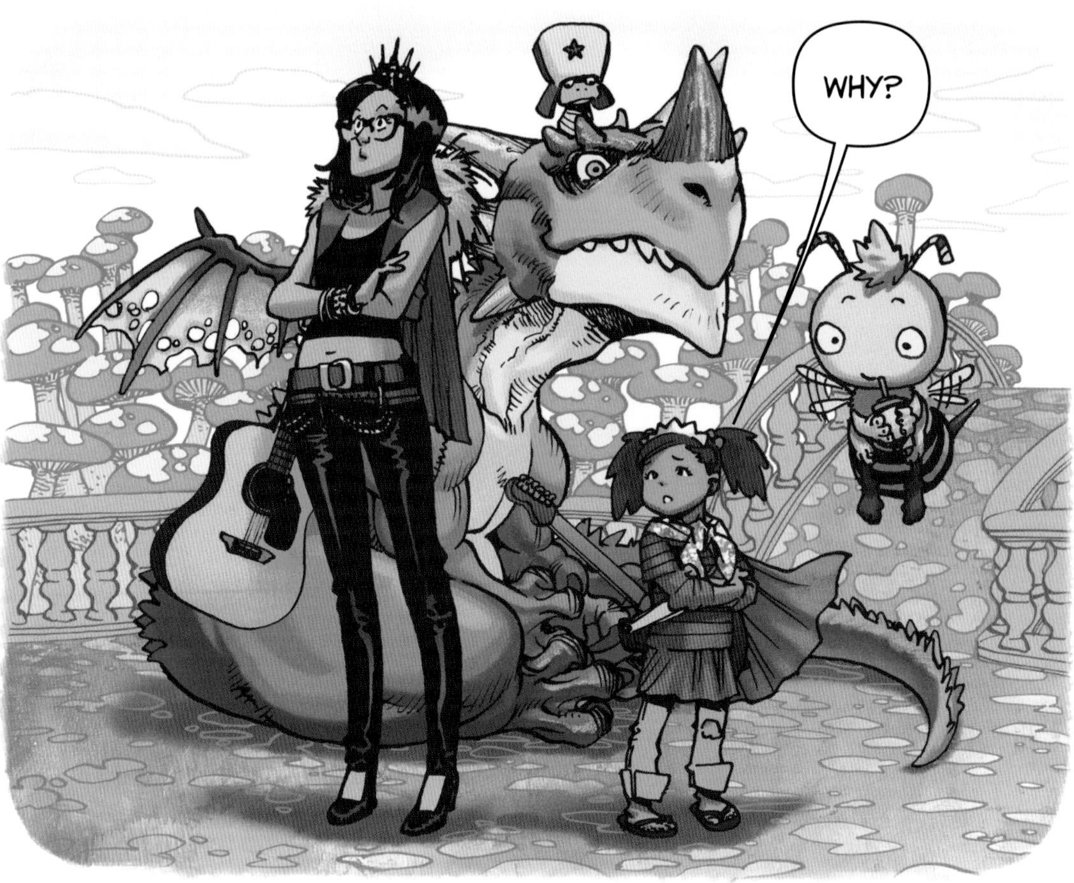
WHY?

And the queen began to cry
And said

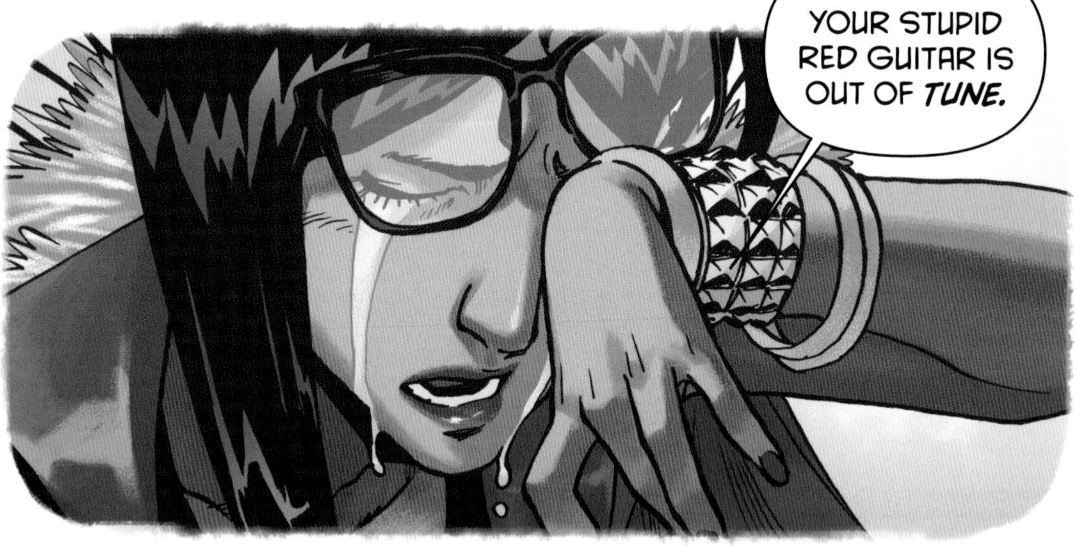
YOUR STUPID RED GUITAR IS OUT OF *TUNE.*

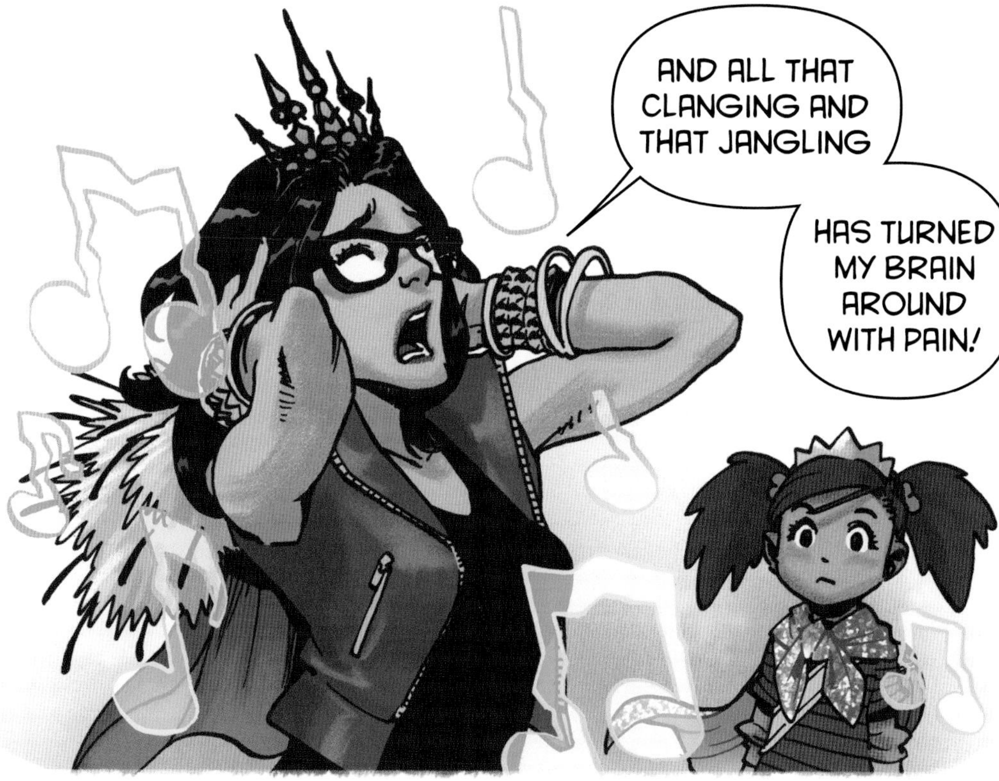
AND ALL THAT CLANGING AND THAT JANGLING
HAS TURNED MY BRAIN AROUND WITH PAIN!

Glory felt her stomach drop.
Like a bubble just went pop.
And she thought of what went wrong

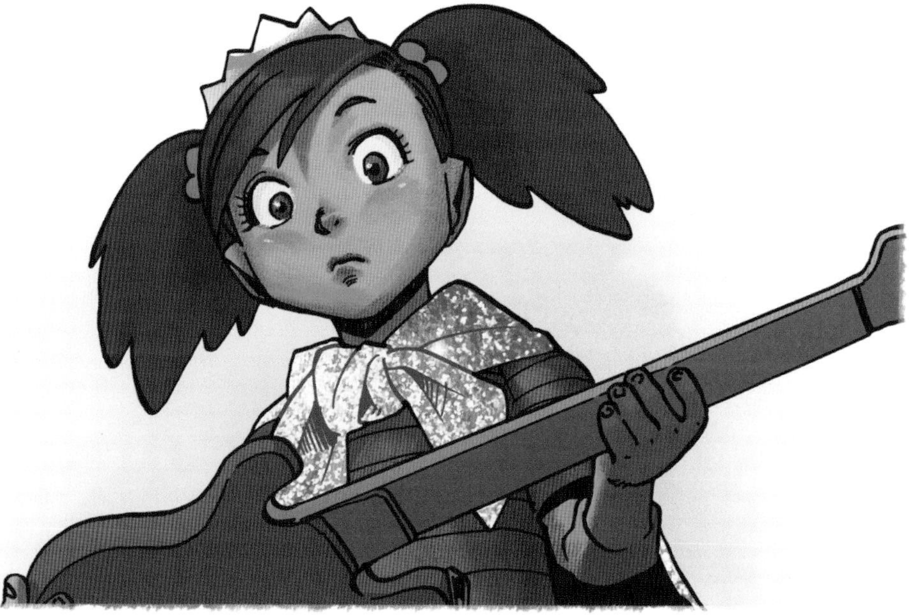

And how on earth to change the song.

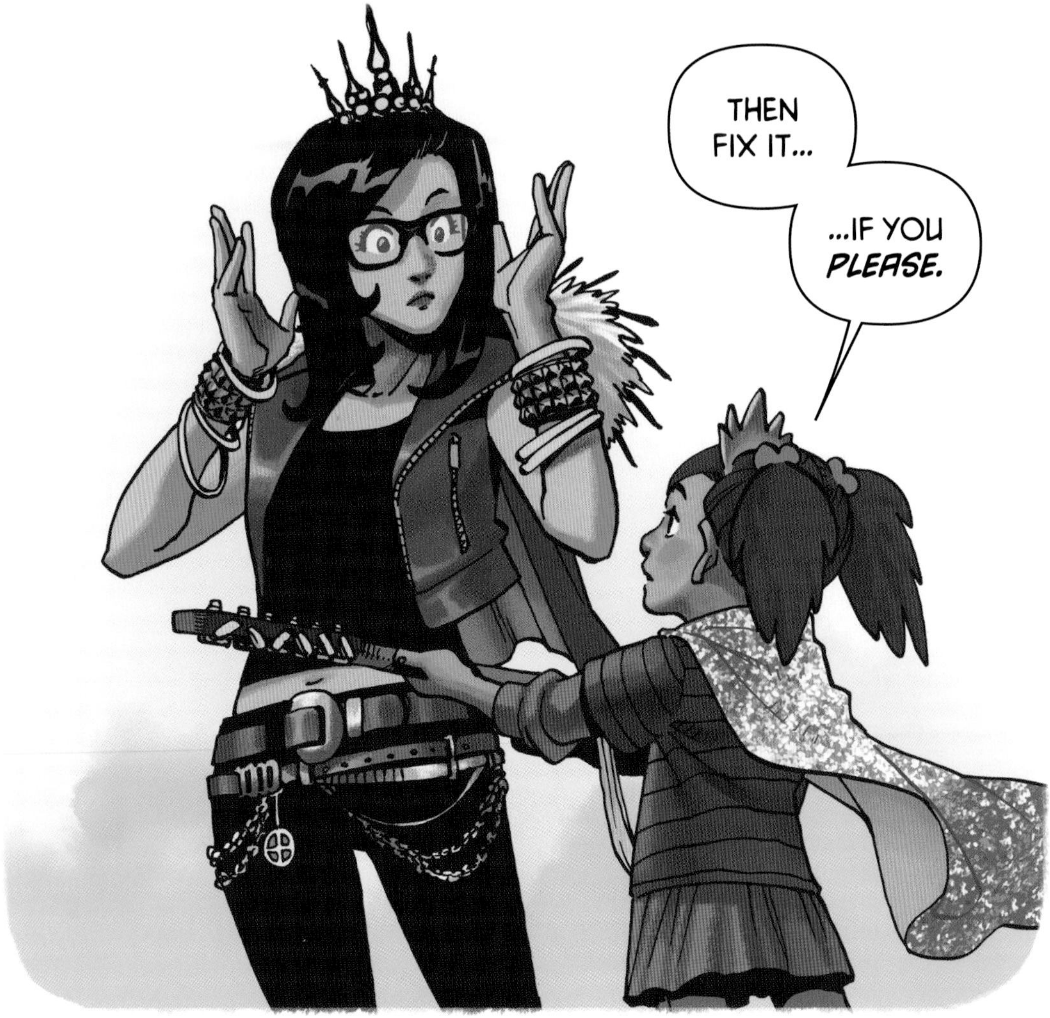
THEN FIX IT...
...IF YOU *PLEASE.*

The queen just stood there in the breeze.

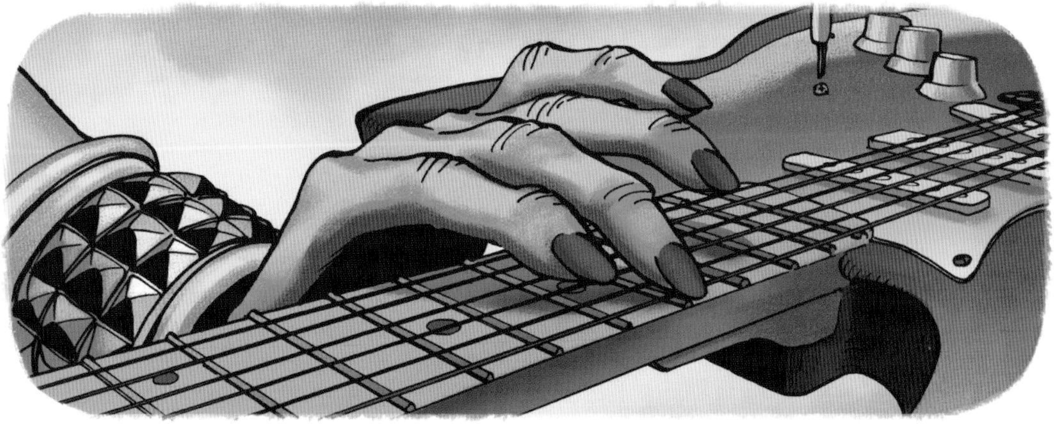

Then reached out with her long claws...

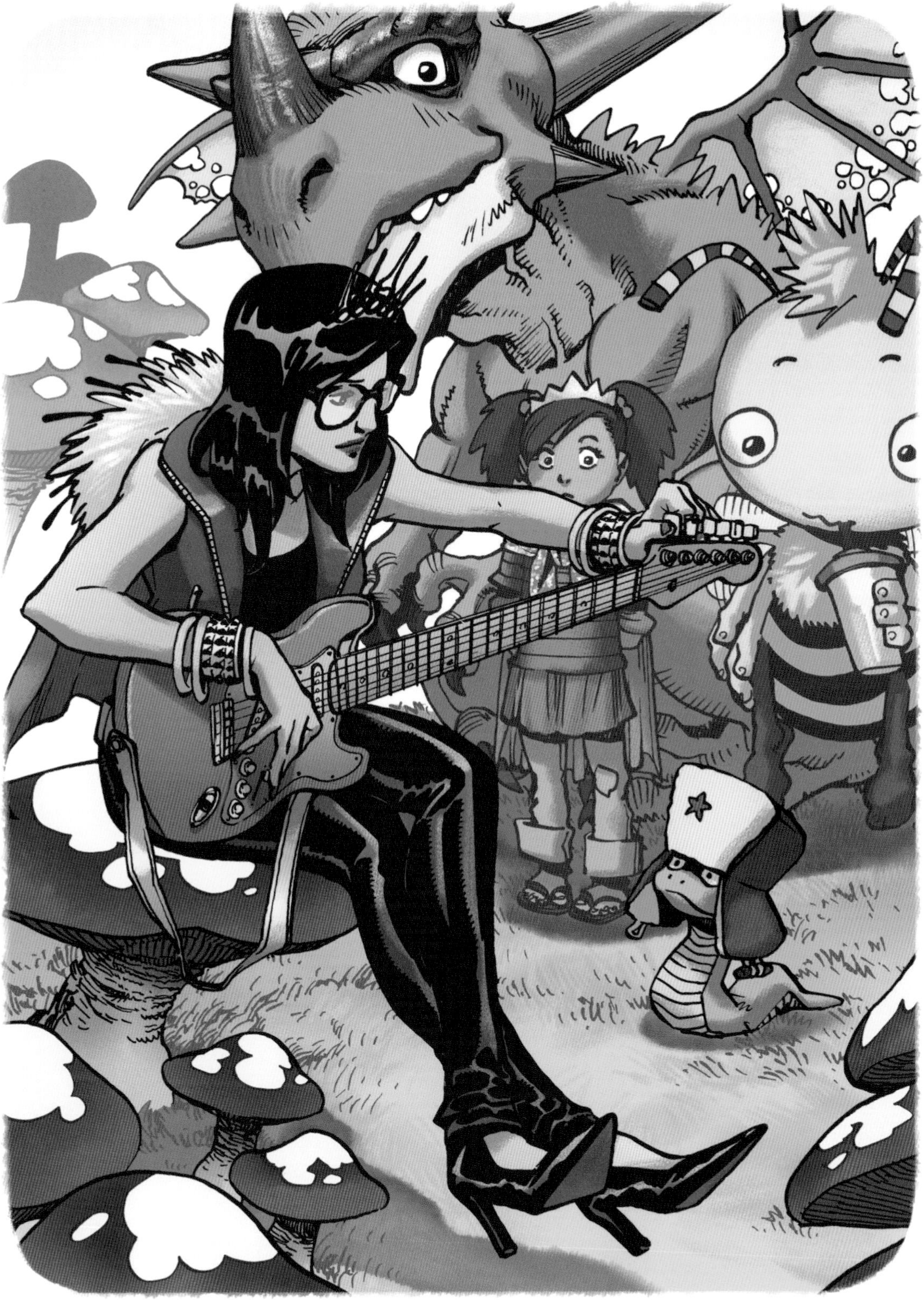

...and slowly tuned our Glory's red guitar.

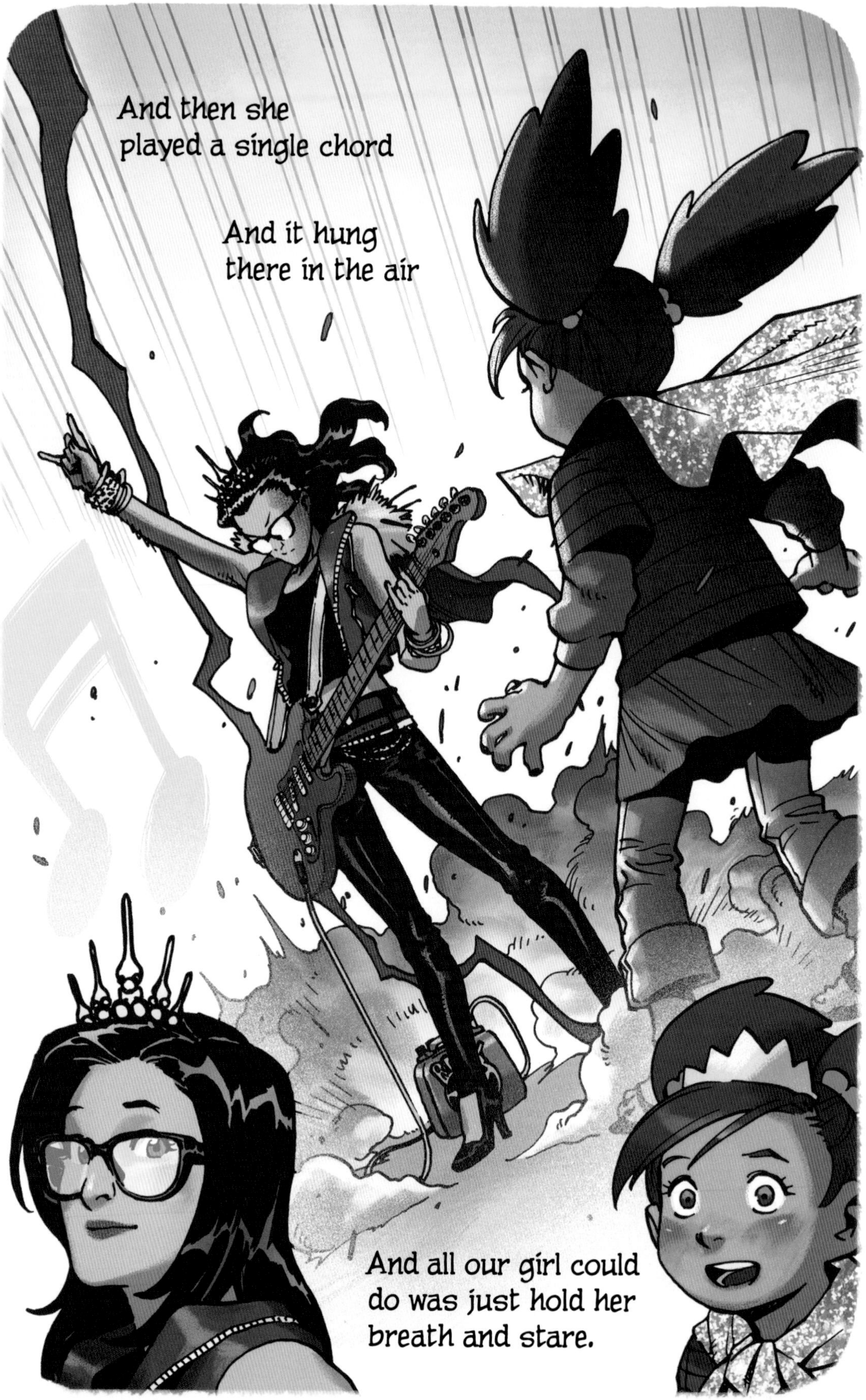
And then she played a single chord
And it hung there in the air
And all our girl could do was just hold her breath and stare.

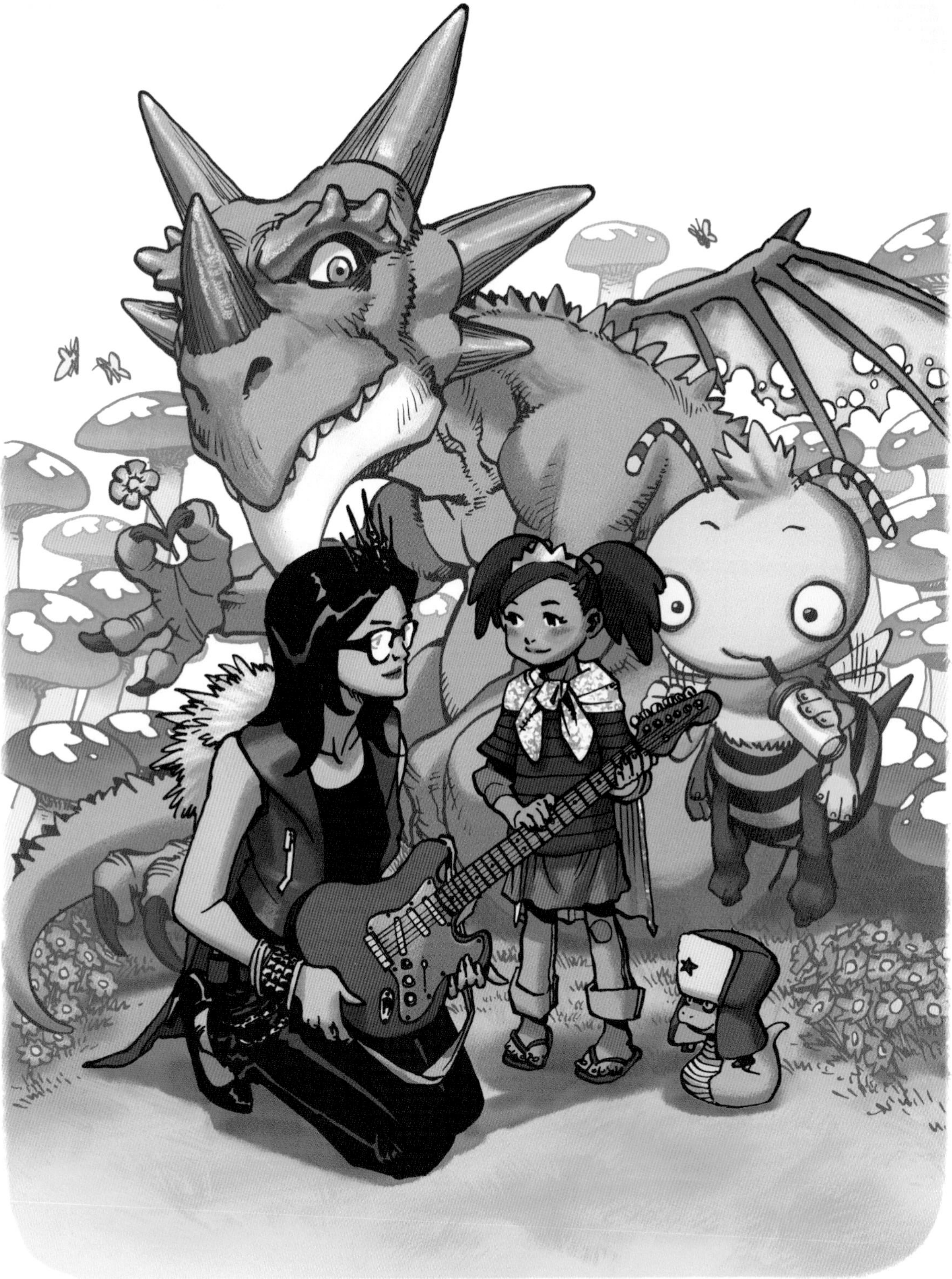

Because she never knew that
her guitar could sound so great.

So they started up a band

And the dragon played the bass

And the princess showed the queen

How to put makeup on her face

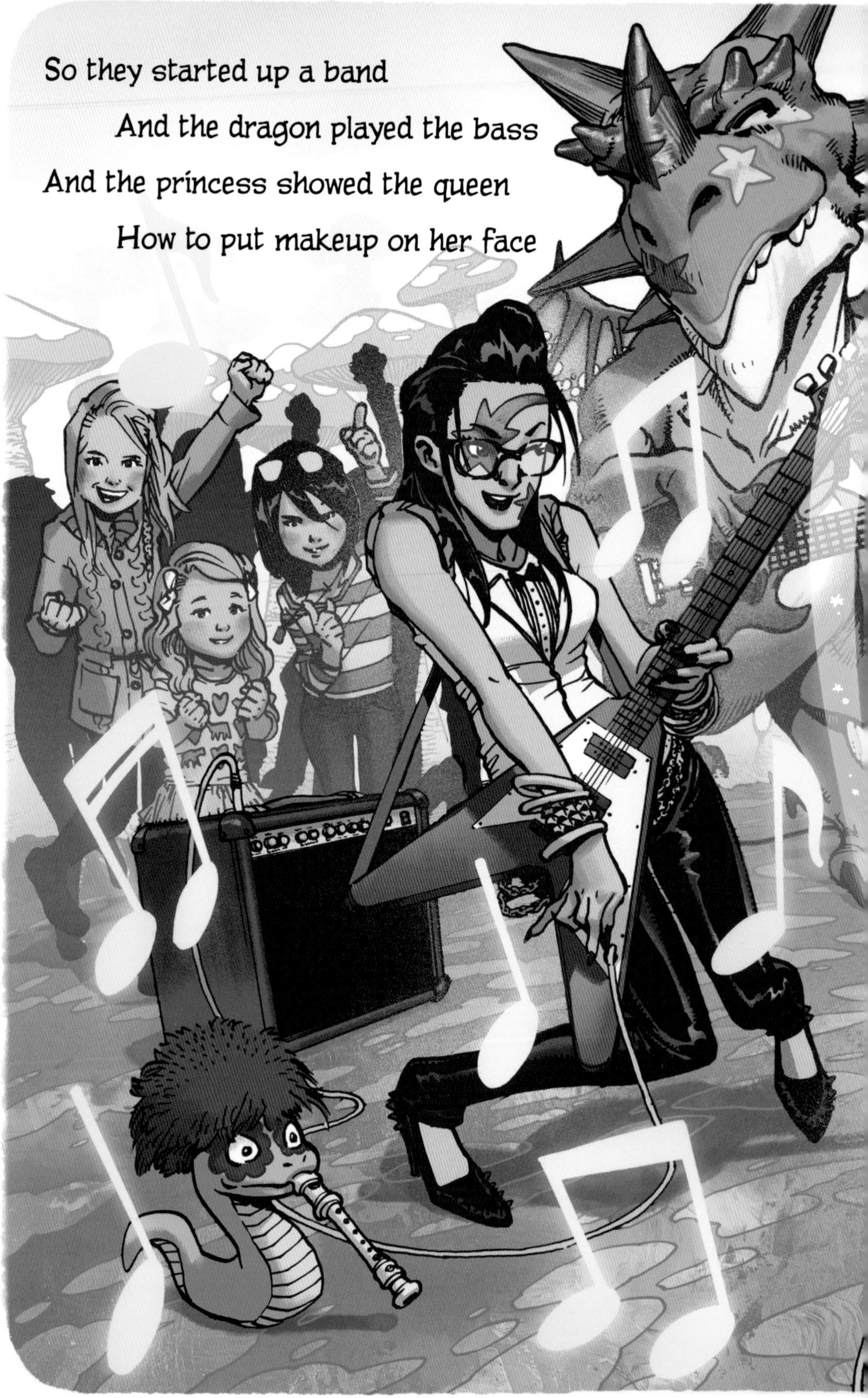

And every day they play

And the kids come out to dance

Because sometimes everyone's a hero

If you just give her a chance.

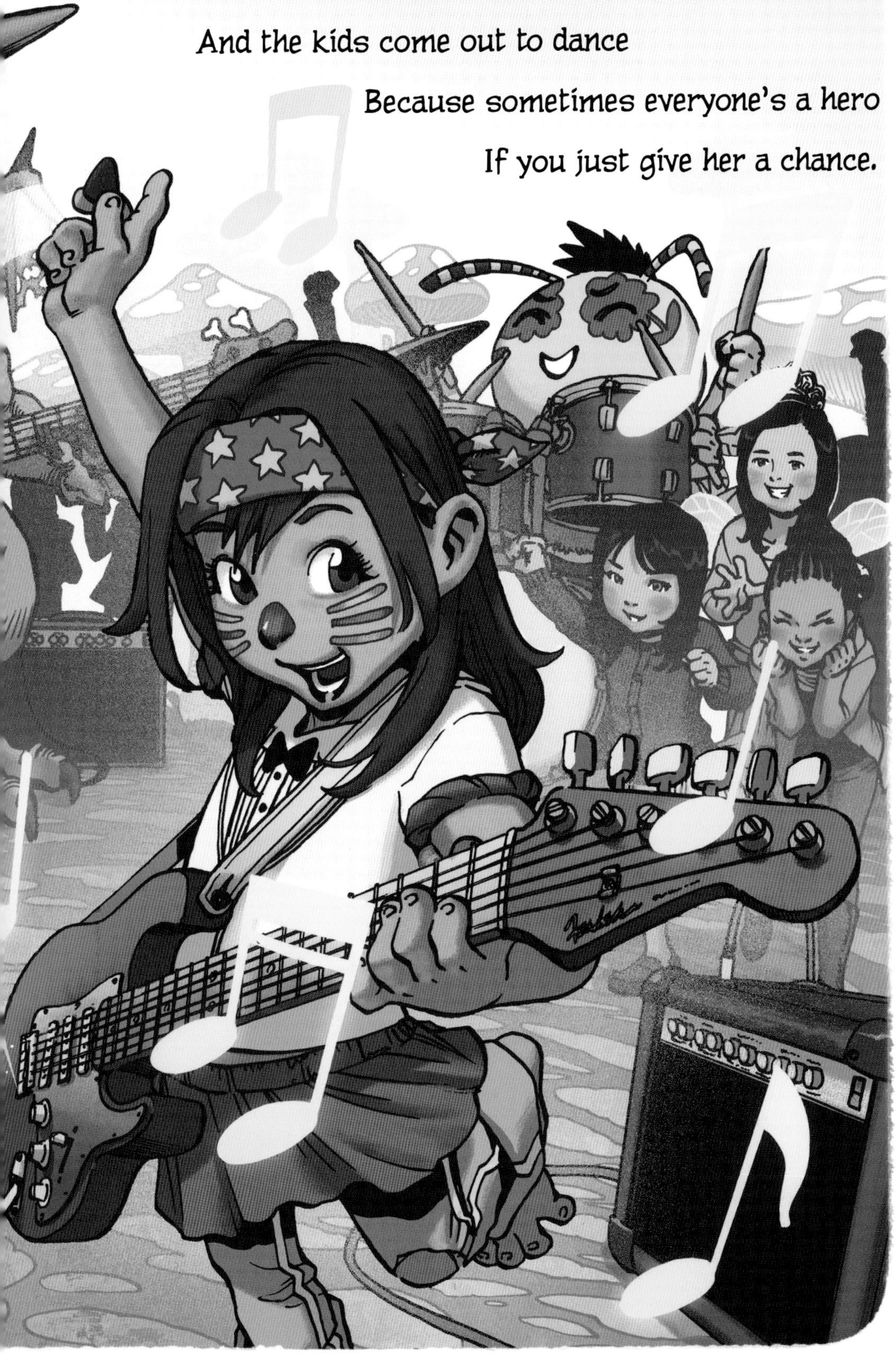

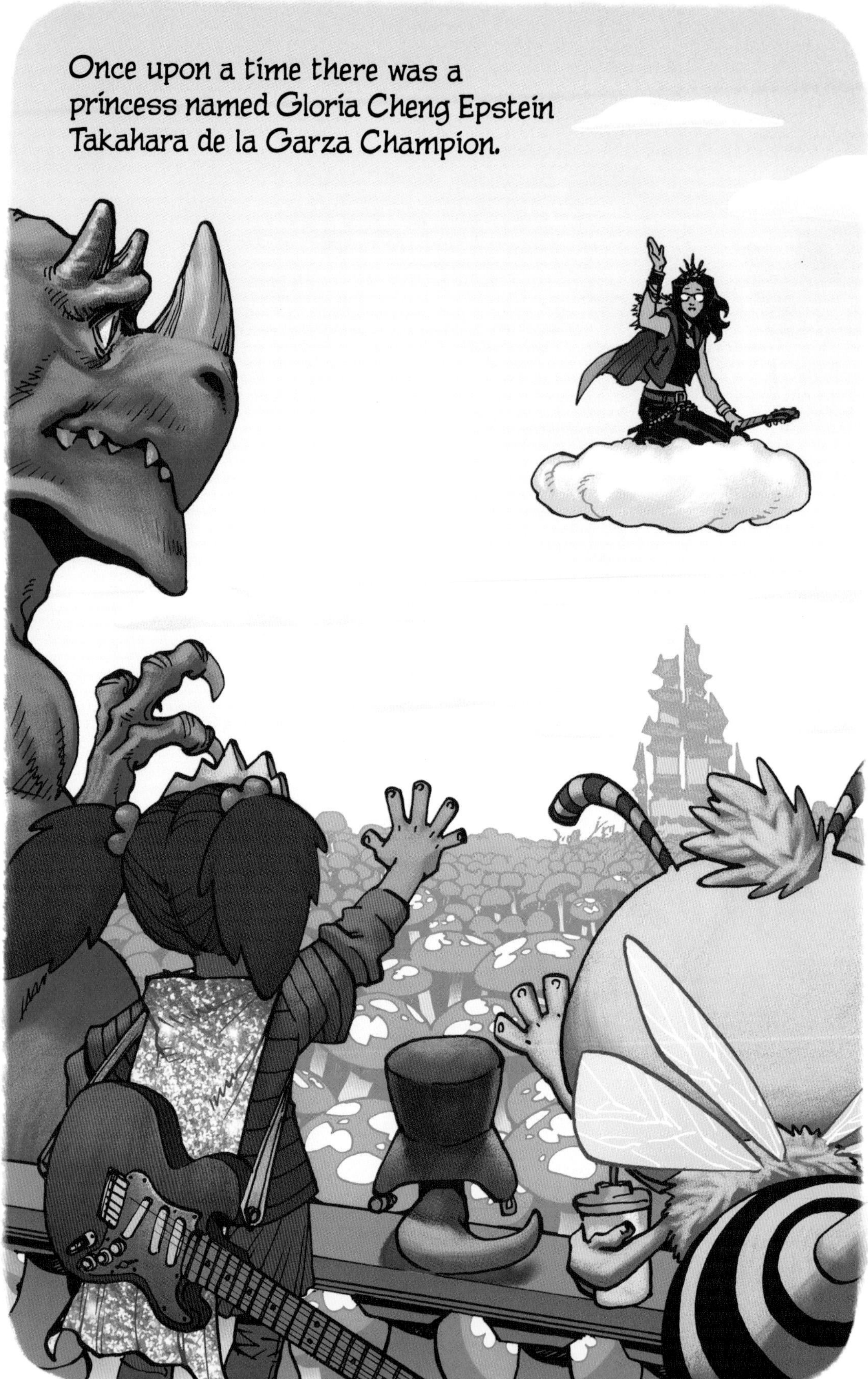
Once upon a time there was a princess named Gloria Cheng Epstein Takahara de la Garza Champion.

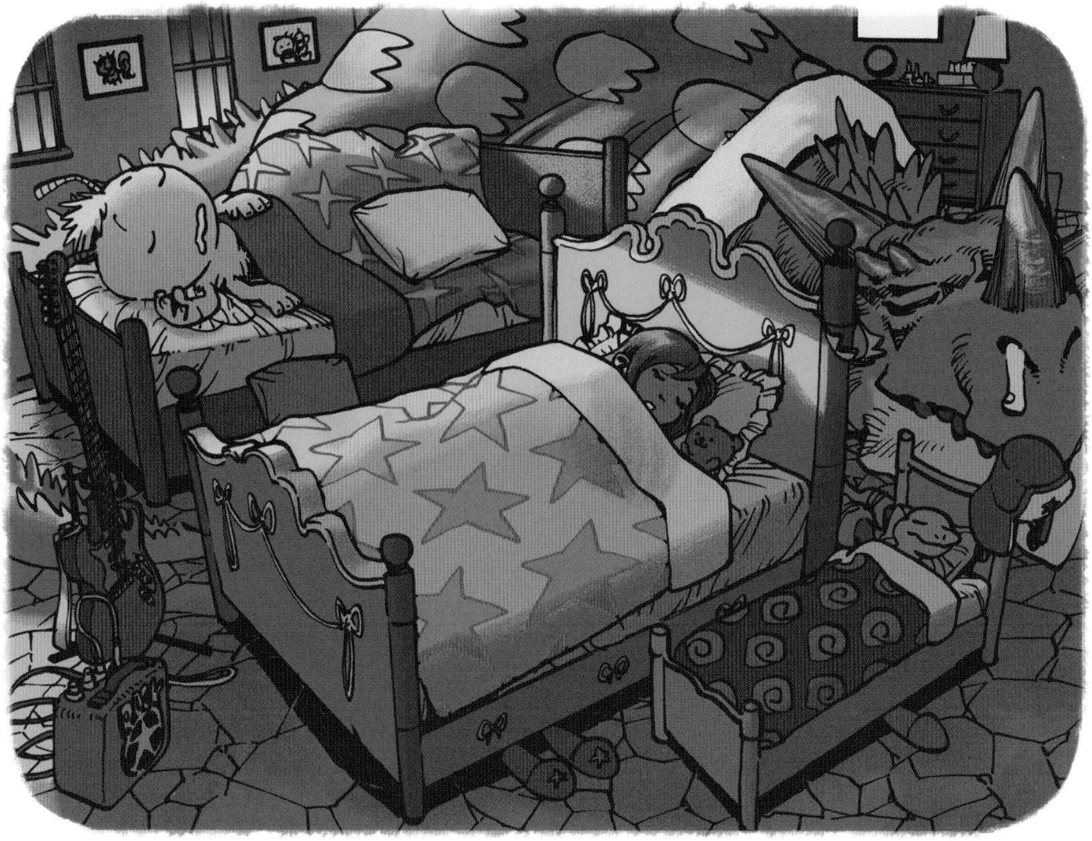

She's my favorite kid

Honest, brave, and true.

But now that I look closely...

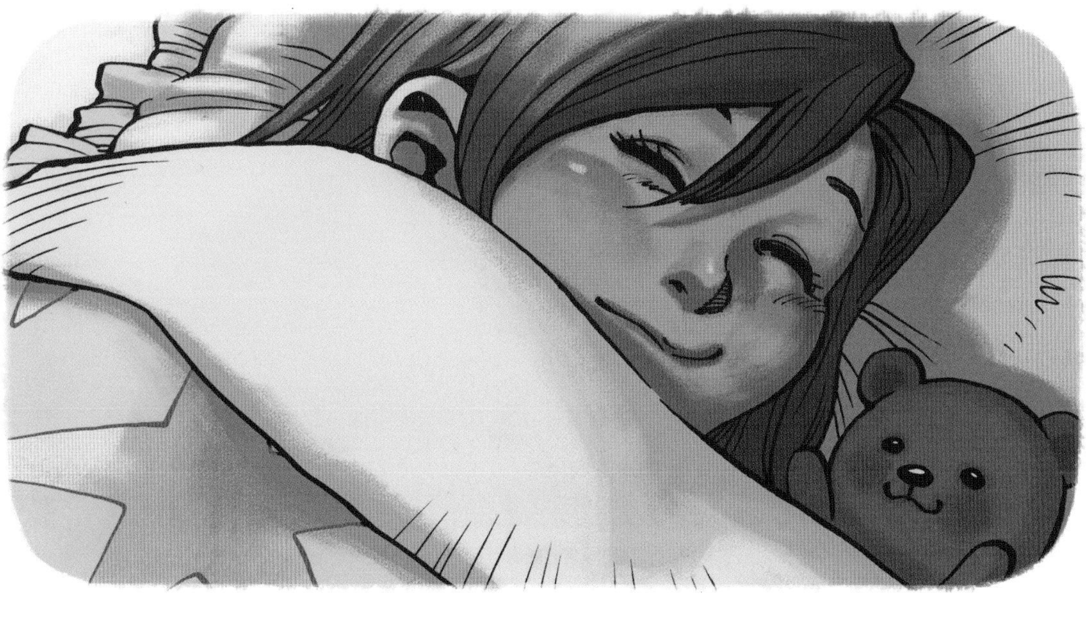

...I think she might be you.

The End.

DISCOVER
# EXPLOSIVE NEW WORLDS

ADVENTURE TIME

Sam Sykes · Selina Espiritu · Sarah Stern
Brave Chef Brianna

KELLY THOMPSON BRIANNE DROUHARD M. VICTORIA ROBADO
MEGA PRINCESS

THE NOT-SO SECRET SOCIETY
DALEY · CRAFTS · CLARK · BRUNI

OVER THE GARDEN WALL

STEVEN UNIVERSE
VOLUME ONE

**Adventure Time**
*Pendleton Ward and Others*
**Volume 1**
ISBN: 978-1-60886-280-1 | $14.99 US
**Volume 2**
ISBN: 978-1-60886-323-5 | $14.99 US
**Adventure Time: Islands**
ISBN: 978-1-60886-972-5 | $9.99 US

**The Amazing World of Gumball**
*Ben Bocquelet and Others*
**Volume 1**
ISBN: 978-1-60886-488-1 | $14.99 US
**Volume 2**
ISBN: 978-1-60886-793-6 | $14.99 US

**Brave Chef Brianna**
*Sam Sykes, Selina Espiritu*
ISBN: 978-1-68415-050-2 | $14.99 US

**Mega Princess**
*Kelly Thompson, Brianne Drouhard*
ISBN: 978-1-68415-007-6 | $14.99 US

**The Not-So Secret Society**
*Matthew Daley, Arlene Daley, Wook Jin Clark*
ISBN: 978-1-60886-997-8 | $9.99 US

**Over the Garden Wall**
*Patrick McHale, Jim Campbell and Others*
**Volume 1**
ISBN: 978-1-60886-940-4 | $14.99 US
**Volume 2**
ISBN: 978-1-68415-006-9 | $14.99 US

**Steven Universe**
*Rebecca Sugar and Others*
**Volume 1**
ISBN: 978-1-60886-706-6 | $14.99 US
**Volume 2**
ISBN: 978-1-60886-796-7 | $14.99 US

**Steven Universe & The Crystal Gems**
ISBN: 978-1-60886-921-3 | $14.99 US

**Steven Universe: Too Cool for School**
ISBN: 978-1-60886-771-4 | $14.99 US

kaboom!™

**AVAILABLE AT YOUR LOCAL COMICS SHOP AND BOOKSTORE**
To find a comics shop in your area, visit www.comicshoplocator.com
WWW.**BOOM-STUDIOS**.COM

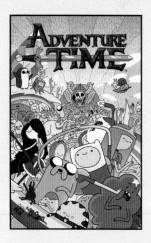

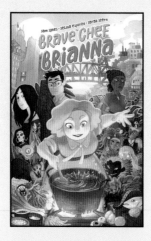

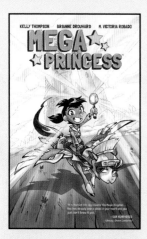

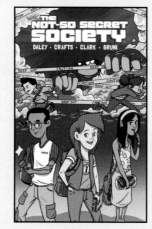

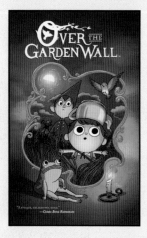

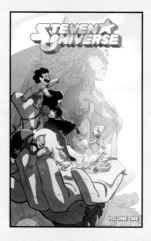

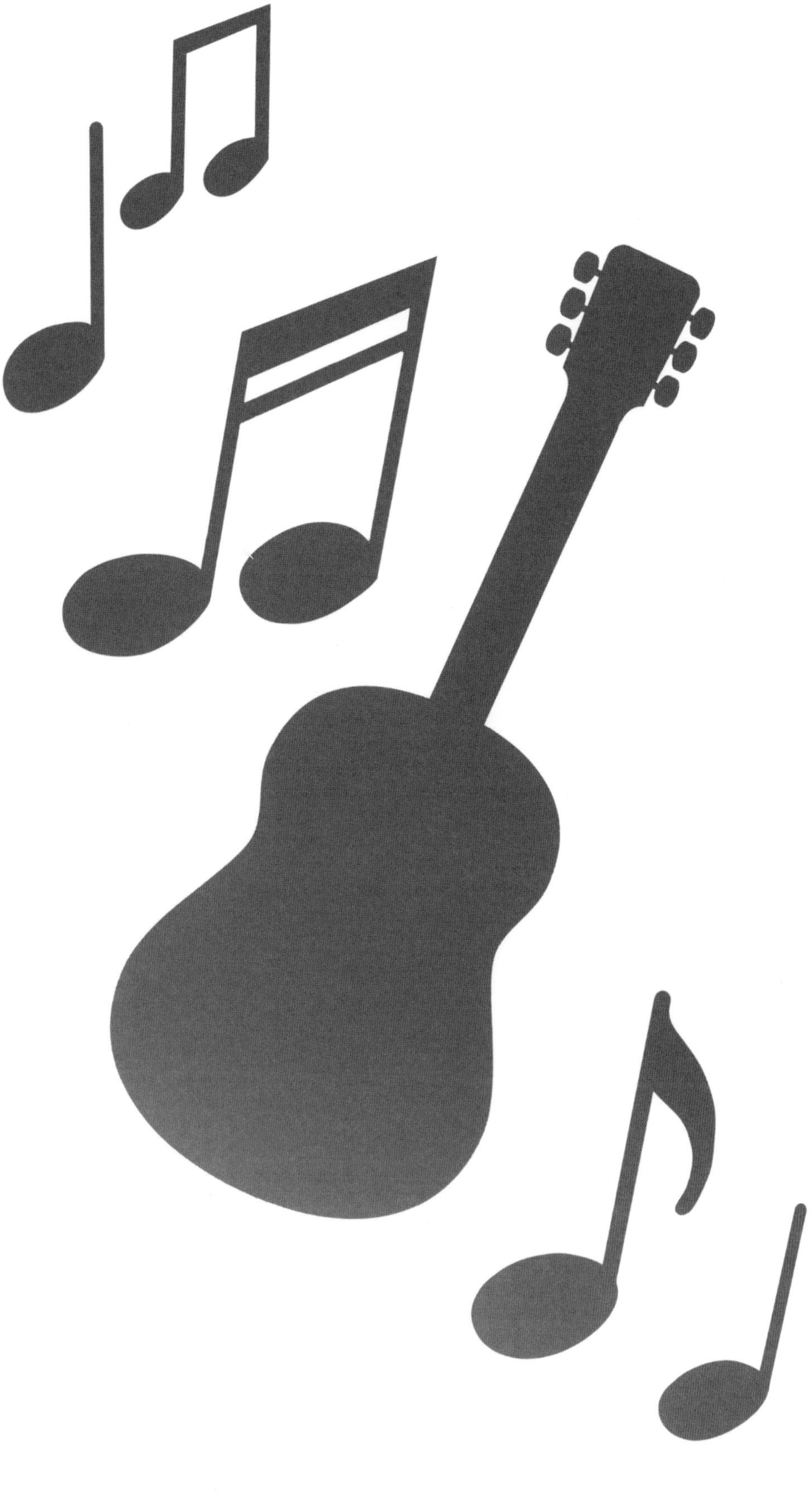